MIDNIGHT CLEAR, TOO

MIRACLE AT MIDNIGHT
BY GWYNNE FORSTER

THE CHOICE
BY MONICA JACKSON

Genesis Press, Inc.

Indigo Love Stories

An imprint of Genesis Press, Inc.
Publishing Company

Genesis Press, Inc.
P.O. Box 101
Columbus, MS 39703

ISBN-13: 978-1-58571-358-5
ISBN-10: 1-58571-358-9
Manufactured in the United States of America

First Edition 2000
Second Edition 2009

Visit us at www.genesis-press.com or call at 1-888-Indigo-1

MIDNIGHT CLEAR, TOO

MIRACLE AT MIDNIGHT

BY GWYNNE FORSTER

They say the old ancestors are still walking the roads here in Mystic, checking on things, watching over folks—like angels, you know. I'd bet money that's what happened with Page and Nelson. Who would have thought those two unlikely folks would have found their way to each other—without some help? Can't say if it was pure coincidence, or something...more. You judge for yourself...

CHAPTER ONE

Nelson Pettiford flipped off the television newscast and blew out a tired breath. Two solid years of electioneering for the presidency, and not one candidate had produced an original idea, he thought. As a political cartoonist, he made his living by exposing politicians to ridicule, but lately the actors on Capitol Hill rarely inspired him. He supplemented his income with his other love—writing novels, which garnered him best sellers. Overall he had a good life, although a lonely one. He got up from his favorite living-room chair and ambled across the hall to his studio, selected some pens and sat down to draw. An hour later, he stood back and surveyed Quigley the cat, his alter ego. A smile flashed over his face as he appraised his work. The big, haughty tomcat gave Odessa-Cat, his onetime girlfriend, the lowdown on the ways in which human beings made life miserable for each other. To Quigley's way of thinking, people could chose incompetent leaders without spending a penny. Yet, every two years, they threw away millions, like bettors at slot machines. He signed the political cartoon as he always did with his pen name, Slim Wisdom, put it in an envelope, drove to the post office and mailed it to the distributor of his syndicated column.

As he left the post office, he stopped and held the door for the woman behind him.

"Thanks," she said, then gazed up at him, grinned and winked. "Wow! How's the weather up there?"

Nelson stared down at the woman until he could see her wince. Why did people feel they had a right to say whatever they thought at the expense of others? When he was in the third grade, he was suspended from school for giving a boy who'd taunted him about his height a reality check. And a harsh one at that. That transgression earned him a lecture from his father on the importance of controlling his temper, and he hadn't forgotten it.

He'd suffered through every insulting name and numerous taunts. Slim, bean pole, skinny, stick. You must be a basketball player. What's the weather forecast? He'd endured the pain of being a spectacle until he'd become inured to it. Men didn't like looking up at other men, so they resorted to ridicule, and women judged him as a man who ought to appreciate any attention they paid him. He'd locked them out, all of them. He walked alone.

On the way home, he took a detour and drove past Lake Linganore as the last rays of the setting sun painted the sky in brilliant hues of red, orange and blue. He'd planned to go straight back home, but he seemed propelled—almost against his will, as if pulled in that direction—to drive past the lake. He drove slowly so as to prolong one of the pleasures of a lonely man, a view of nature at its most majestic.

Page Sutherland pressed the accelerator to the floor, then pumped the gas a few times. Nothing. Four o'clock on a chilly October afternoon on a strange road, an isolated road, and her car wouldn't move. She'd had a tune-up the previous week and filled the tank with gas less than fifty miles back and, apart from driving a car, that was all she knew to do to one. Strange. The car had just stopped without a warning. Not a change in the engine or locked brakes. Nothing. The thought of getting out of the car in that out-of-the-way spot sent cold prickles from her neck to the base of her spine. Even if she were willing to risk walking, she had no idea how far it was to Mystic Ridge. She'd been huddled in the car for all of forty-five minutes when she saw the headlights of the approaching car.

The sight of a Chevy parked on the other side of the highway got Nelson's attention, and he stopped and crossed the two-lane roadway to where a lone woman huddled in the front seat. As he approached, she rolled up the window.

"Are you all right?" he asked her. "Can I help you in some way?"

Something, maybe it was fear, or it could have been caution, mirrored in her eyes. The eyes of a woman in jeopardy, or who believed she was. He stared down at her long-lashed dreamy eyes, framed in a flawless brown face, and inexplicably connected with her from his scalp to the pit of his gut.

"Well?"

She shook her head. "Uh…No. Fine," he thought she said, though he couldn't be sure because she didn't roll down the window.

"You're sure you're all right?"

She nodded so vigorously that he didn't believe her, but what could he do? In the circumstances, any intelligent woman would be wary. He turned away and walked back to his car, but he didn't like leaving her there. He didn't like it one bit.

Maybe she should have trusted him, but how could she go off with a stranger on that deserted road in the encroaching darkness? His was the only car she'd seen in the last hour or so. And who was he? She didn't think she'd ever seen such a tall man. Dark, elegant and handsome, too. As uneasy as she was out there alone, he could have been an illusion, an image she conjured up. Still…Something moved in the thicket beside the highway, or so she thought. She checked the windows and the locks on the doors. Another movement, this time closer to her. Her breathing accelerated and she rubbed her moist hands. The night sounds began in earnest, as crickets chirped out an anthem and frogs began to croak in a seesaw rhythm. A far-away boom with the sound of roaring thunder split the silence, and she wrapped her arms around her body.

In a brief flash of lightning, she caught a glimpse of the most exquisite looking rust-colored tom cat sitting regally on the road. In a blink, the cat was gone. Page burrowed deeper in the seat, a sensation of the surreal filling her. Yet, she felt perfectly safe, even as she wondered what she'd gotten herself into.

Six hours earlier—it felt like six years—she'd set out from Washington, D.C. looking for a life of her own, away from her mother's career, popularity and maddening social life. A journalist, she'd accepted a position as reporter for a weekly paper in Mystic Ridge and a chance to be her own person. If she made friends and succeeded as a journalist, it would at least be the result of her own efforts and abilities and not because she was Millie Shipley's daughter. And she'd be away from her glamorous mother's notoriety and have a life of her own. She and her mother loved each other, but they were as different as two women could be. She'd left Washington glowing with expectation as to what might happen in her new life, but so far she was batting zero. Thunder crashed and bellowed closer this time, and she lay down in the seat, frightened by the sound of dogs barking nearby. *Probably after that poor cat.*

The headlights of a motor vehicle lit up her car, and she sat up with such suddenness that her head hit the steering wheel. Fear shot through her as a pickup truck parked across the highway and the driver's door opened, but her heartbeat slowed to normal when she recognized the tall man. He'd come back, and somehow she knew he wouldn't harm her. If he'd wanted to, he could have done that two hours earlier. She opened the window a crack.

"It's too dangerous for you to spend the night out here," he said. "If you're afraid of me, you can stay in your car, and I'll tow you to Mystic Ridge. If you won't do that, I'll just sit across there in my truck to make sure nobody bothers you, but I can't leave you alone out here."

Lightning streaked through the sky and shivers raced through her. It was silly, she knew, but lightning always made her uneasy. Maybe...

She rolled down the window. "I...uh..." If she didn't go with him, she could become someone else's victim. "If you'll tow my car, I'll ride with you. I'm headed for Mystic Ridge."

"Well, go sit in the truck before it begins to rain."

She liked his voice. Strong and authoritative. A voice that commanded respect. She did as he suggested, and she'd never been more grateful than when he got in the truck, made a U-turn and got out without touching her. He succeeded in hooking her car to the truck as drops of rain began to fall.

"Where're you staying in Mystic?"

"I was going to the Ridgewood Inn, but it's already nine-thirty, and it's probably full."

"Mystic Ridge is a small place and it isn't a tourist attraction. So your room will be there for you."

· He stopped in front of the Ridgewood Inn. "I'll help you with your things."

She noticed that the receptionist stared from her to the tall man, and Page hastened to waylay any suggestion that she might be checking in with him.

"I reserved a single room and bath for today, but I had engine trouble. I hope you still have the room."

The woman nodded, though she stared at the man who'd proved to be Page's salvation.

"You're all right now," he said to her. "I'll leave your car out front."

She turned to thank him, but he strode out of the door, and when she followed him, he stopped, turned and said, "I'm glad you're safe. Goodbye."

The sharp finality of his tone stunned her, leaving her with no choice but to walk back into the hotel.

"What is that man's name?" she asked the receptionist. "Do you know who he is?"

"Me?" the woman asked, pointing to her chest. " 'Deed I don't know a thing about that man. People say he's strange, but don't ask me."

Frowning, Page went to her room, ordered a chicken breast sandwich, ate it, showered and went to bed. And when she closed her eyes, she saw again the face of the tall man who rescued her.

A week later, having found a suitable house and settled into her new job at *The Mystic Ridge Observer,* Page focused on finding a niche for herself in the place she hoped would become her home. Already, she had a sense of freedom and of opportunity to find out who she was and what she could do away from the glare, commotion and excitement that continually surrounded her mother.

But first, she had to find the man and thank him. She described the man to the handyman who worked around the neighboring houses. "Do you know who he is?"

"Well, I've seen him, ma'am, but people say he doesn't talk to anybody. I'm not even sure he can talk, and they say he's weird, too. Stays in a big house with a high fence and they say he's got ten or fifteen bad dogs in there. Must be hiding from the law is all I can say."

She didn't know about the dogs, but the rest of it was off the mark. She questioned Phyllis, the copy editor at *The Observer,* as the local folk called it.

"What you want to know about him for? He's some kind of hermit. Walks around looking straight ahead and ignoring everybody like they say witches do. People here have gotten used to him, but nobody knows where he came from. You'd think the wind would blow him over, he's so tall." She chuckled at her own joke.

Page had had enough of the speculations. Living in a small town had some disadvantages, and ruinous gossip topped the list. "Where does he live?"

"Last house on Fritchie Road going toward Frederick. It's practically on the spot where Barbara

Fritchie is supposed to have stonewalled old Stonewall Jackson himself when he marched through these parts during the Civil War. Why do you want to know anyway?"

"I'm a reporter, and all this stuff I hear about him has piqued my curiosity."

"Oh yeah? Well, you might as well forget about an interview. That man don't talk to nobody."

"Did I hear you asking about that string bean out on Fritchie Road?" James Rodgers, editor of *The Observer,* asked, as he knocked and walked into the office Page shared with Phyllis. "You know him?" Page explained how they met. "Doesn't sound like the same guy, but if it is and you get to meet him, I want a story." She promised to do her best. Her curiosity at fever pitch, she made up her mind to visit him the following day. When she awoke that morning, Saturday, Nelson Pettiford was her first thought. Around noon, she dressed to go to his house, but decided she'd better call her mother first.

It seemed as if a hundred people talking at once stood directly behind her mother when she answered the phone. "Oh, darling, I'm just having a few people over for lunch. I owe everybody, and in this town, that's not good. As a member of the House of Representatives, I can be powerful and make a difference or I can be as useful as a wet match. Darling, how are you?"

"Me?" asked Page, winded by the speed at which her mother's words flew out. "I'm fine. I called to see how you are."

"Never better, darling. You know me. I'd planned to call and remind you of the Urban League gala. I can't go to that place alone, and I hate being obligated to these excuses for men. Look, I have to go. Senator Lucus just arrived."

Same old, same old. "Love you." She hung up. It wasn't ever going to change.

CHAPTER TWO

Nelson dashed out of the house and down to the gate when he recognized Mr. Whitfield's buzz. The man had a special way of pushing the buzzer. One, three, two, one buzzes, so he always knew when his mail had arrived.

"Morning, Mr. Whitfield. You're late today. I was afraid something had happened to you."

Whitfield removed his government regulation blue postman's hat and scratched his head. "I had to get signatures on a lot of packages, and you can't just hand Miss Laura a letter, she has to talk for half an hour. I don't mind, though, 'cause I'm the only person she gets to talk with. Here's your mail."

"Thanks." Miss Laura wasn't alone. Whitfield was often the only person to whom he spoke for days, so he understood the woman's reluctance to let the man continue his rounds. "See you tomorrow," he said and turned back to the house, but before he reached halfway the buzzer sounded again.

Now, who could that be? He wasn't expecting his brother, Logan, and his only other visitor was the man who took care of his house. The buzzing persisted. Instead of speaking over the intercom, he walked out to the gate and stopped dead in his tracks. It couldn't be. She'd stayed in his head, lived in his dreams and frolicked in and out of his thoughts since that night when she'd taken over his life. He walked closer. Her radiant smile changed to a grin. Excitement raced through him.

"Hi. It's me, the woman you rescued on Old Mills Road the other night. I had to find you and thank you. It wasn't easy, either."

He walked all the way to the gate, looked into her long-lashed, brownish gray eyes and felt her sink into him and burrow her way into his soul. He shook his head to clear it, to retrieve himself, but she was in him, he knew it.

She sniffed. "What do I smell that's so tantalizing?"

"Forgive me," he managed. "I must seem rude. I'm roasting chestnuts that I gathered from my tree this morning. They're wonderful. Would you..." He hesitated. If she said no or acted as if she was turned off by him, he didn't think he could bear it.

"Would I what? Like some chestnuts? I warn you, I love them."

He unlocked the gate and opened it, scared that she'd hear his heart pounding. "Would you like to come in? I've got a fire around back where I'm roasting the nuts, and it's warm there."

"Thanks. My name is Page Sutherland. You didn't tell me yours, and nobody seems to know it."

Something akin to empathy surfaced in her eyes, and she stopped herself as she nearly grasped his arm.

He took the hand she extended. Soft and feminine. "I'm Nelson Pettiford."

Recognition of the name seemed to flicker in her eyes, but to his relief, all she said was, "Thank you for being so kind to me the other night. It's something I'll never forget."

He shrugged. "I'm glad I came back for you."

She walked beside him, obviously at ease, and he recognized in himself an expansive feeling, a sensation of belonging with someone. A feeling as alien to him as any he could imagine. He breathed deeply, and allowed himself to enjoy it, if only for a little while.

"Have a seat," he said, pointing to one of the lounge chairs that he kept there. He hooded his eyes and watched her. More than once, he'd seen people run from him, but she didn't hesitate to take a seat and, in almost slow motion, crossed the shapeliest pair of legs he'd seen in years.

"What a soothing environment! And the music. I love Mozart's chamber music."

He stopped turning the nuts and looked steadily at her. "I could listen to it twenty-four hours a day and never get tired of it. I like other music, but I need this. I don't know how I could get along without it for long."

She leaned back and closed her eyes. "It's wonderful. I like jazz when I'm doing chores around the house, and I love opera, but this makes me feel alive."

The tongs fell from his hand down to the hot coals, but he paid no attention. Had fate, or an angel, sent her to him? Or was this another of the strange happenings in his life since some force beyond himself had pulled him onto Old Mills Road where she sat stranded. He didn't believe in coincidences anymore than he believed in predestination, but from the minute he'd first looked into her eyes, he'd lost himself. Over a week later, nothing had changed that. She smiled, and he knew he'd been staring at her.

"What is it?" she asked.

He raked the tongs away from the coals with a stick. "I don't remember having been so comfortable with anyone as I am with you, except maybe my brother. It's been…I don't know…maybe never. Don't tell me you like walking in the woods."

A smile drifted over her face, mesmerizing him. "All right. I won't. But I will say that, during summer camp, I spent many hours in the woods. As a child, I couldn't wait for spring, so I could do my studying in a tree in our garden. I'm a card-carrying nature lover."

He peeled the roasted chestnuts, gave her some in a small bowl and watched her eyes blaze with delight as she anticipated eating them. "Are you warm enough? I could get you a sweater or a blanket."

"I'm fine. The fire is wonderful, and I enjoy looking at the flames. They're like puppets dancing to an imaginary tune. Central heating has its draw-backs."

"I have central heating, but I also have fireplaces in most rooms. They make it so much more....well, like home."

He glanced down at her feet. When had he seen anybody tap their toes to Mozart's music? What an inviting woman! He realized he could care a lot for her and checked himself. He didn't know her, and he didn't plan to lose his heart to any woman only to regret it.

Page leaned back, savored the delicious nuts and considered Nelson Pettiford. Thoughtful. Kind. It hadn't occurred to her that he'd peel those hot chest-nuts so she could eat them while they were warm. She wanted to ask him why the townspeople had such peculiar opinions of him when nothing they'd told her about him bore any semblance of the truth, but she sensed he'd shut her out if she put him on the defen-sive. Weird? Definitely not. His handsome brown face boasted the dreamiest eyes she remembered looking at. And she liked his mouth, too. Firm lips. Not too thin and not too...She sat forward. What was she doing lolling there fantasizing about a strange man?

"It's been a wonderful few minutes, Nelson, but I'd better go." When he looked at his watch, and a half smile formed around his lips, she looked at her own watch.

"Good Lord, I've been here almost three hours." She frowned, confused. "But how could that be? I didn't intend to…You've wasted a whole afternoon with me—"

"This afternoon was not wasted. It was…something very special."

She stood, and he got up immediately and walked down to the gate with her. If she'd had the nerve to do what she wanted, she would have kissed his cheek in gratitude for the most pleasant afternoon she could remember. Instead, she thanked him again, shook hands with him and left.

He watched her car until it turned the corner. *Yes, I felt it too, Page, that sensation of being lost in time, transported somehow.* He shook his head, dispelling the weird notion, and returned to the grill. He stood there gazing at it for long minutes. Its flames still crackled, Mozart's music continued to fill the air with romance and the aroma of the chestnuts still clung to his nostrils, but he doused the fire, stopped the music and went inside. The awful emptiness. He pushed it back, sat down at his drawing table and got to work. Damned if he'd let it beat him.

"Did you get anything good on Pettiford?" James Rodgers asked Page the following Monday morning.

She couldn't lie, but she wouldn't betray Nelson, either. "You said he wouldn't see me, didn't you? Don't tell me you came in here to gloat."

"Truth is I didn't hold out much hope for it, but since you're new in town and didn't know anything about him…" He let the thought hang, shrugged and went back to his office.

"I'm not gloating, either," Phyllis sang out.

Page locked her computer, dusted her keyboard and considered ignoring Phyllis, but she wanted to prove she could make friends on her own, so she said to her office mate, "I'll give you a little of my late father's philosophy: don't expect too much of your friends, and you'll always have them. The boss didn't expect anything, and he's not disappointed."

"Yeah," Phyllis drawled, "but if you'd gotten that interview, he'd be dancing on the ceiling."

"Can't you just see those bowed legs tripping over each other while he does a two-step on the ceiling? I'm going to the City Council meeting. See you tomorrow."

"Right."

Page grabbed her briefcase and camera, dashed out of the building and stopped as she opened the door of her car. "Hmmm." Something could be going on there. Phyllis never made jokes about James and didn't comment if anybody else did. Boredom quickly overtook her during the Council meeting and her mind drifted back to the previous Saturday afternoon and the idyllic moments with Nelson. She'd thought only of him since she'd left his house, flustered by her easy acceptance of him. She'd actually closed her eyes, relaxed and daydreamed while he sat less than four feet from her. She didn't care what the gossips said; she trusted him because her instincts said she should and, so far, he'd proved worthy of it.

Why couldn't she see him again? He didn't suggest it, and she knew he wouldn't. She wanted to spend time with him, to know him. She suspected he was the same Nelson Pettiford who'd written three national best-selling novels, but if he wanted her to know that, he'd tell her. And the longer he kept it to himself, the more attractive he'd be. If there was anything she could do without, it was another seeker of notoriety. Life with her headline-grabbing mother, as much as she loved her, had erased her tolerance for people who needed the spotlight. She fished in her pocketbook for a quarter, went to the phone and called him. She reached his answering machine.

"Mr. Pettiford," she said, speaking to the answering machine, "this is Page Sutherland. I'm sorry you're not at home. I hate talking to these infernal things. I'll—"

"Hello, Page. I can't imagine a more pleasant surprise or a more welcome one. But how'd you get my number?"

"Bribery. The boss' sister works for the phone company, and I promised her dinner if she'd give me your number. I hope you don't mind. I…I spent such a wonderful afternoon with you that I…Well, I don't know anyone else whose company suited me like…Oh, for goodness sake, Nelson, can't we see each other again?"

"Do you…Yes. Yes, I want to see you. I've hardly thought of anything else since you left here. What's your phone number, and what time do you get home?"

Her heart started a shaky waltz in her chest, and she took a deep breath and leaned against the side of the building. "711-1177. I'll be there about four-thirty," she managed to say. What was it about the man's voice? It seemed to soothe her, to wrap her in a dreamy kind of peace.

"If you're free for dinner this evening, we can talk about it when I call you. Around six?"

"If you're just being a gentleman, I want to know it right now, and I'll excuse you."

"Ha ha." His laughter had the ring of honest relief. "I'm thirty-six, Page, so unless someone needs my help, I'm not likely to agree to do something I don't want to do. I'd like to see you, and I've already begun to anticipate the pleasure of being with you again."

Oh, dear. This one didn't let any weeds grow under his feet. "Till then."

"Right. Call you at six."

She hung up and made herself walk the half block to her car. Where had she gotten the nerve to call a strange man and tell him she wanted to see him again? His immediate response was more than she'd hoped for, but she definitely wasn't going to make a habit of seeking him out.

What should she wear to dinner with him? If she were in Washington, she'd go for broke, but women in

Mystic Ridge didn't seem to dress up except on special occasions. She'd wait till he called and take her cue from him.

~~~

Nelson propped his elbows on his drawing table, leaned forward and rested his face in his hands. If this was a joke, he couldn't find the humor in it. The phone rang and his head snapped up. He stared at the phone and let it ring. Was she calling to say she'd acted on impulse?

"I thought you said you'd be home this evening, and—"

He grabbed the phone, flipped off the answering machine and interrupted his brother. "Good grief! I did, didn't I? But—"

"Look, man, if you gotta go somewhere, I can take a rain check. No problem."

He'd forgotten that his brother planned to spend the night with him, as he did once every two or three weeks. "It's okay. I…uh…I forgot about it. But come on over. You have a key, so let yourself in. I'll…uh…I ought to be back around ten."

He heard the silence on the other end of the wire and waited, knowing that Logan would place his shots accurately.

"Who's the girl?" Logan's deep baritone always seemed to come from the pit of his belly. Although two inches shorter than he, Logan had always seemed bigger, for he wore the aura of strength that a boy finds in an older brother. His good looks made him a favorite with women, but he was a man who did his own choosing.

"Not anyone I care to talk about. I just met her," Nelson said.

"I see. When and where?"

Nelson allowed himself a hearty laugh. "The eighteen months difference in our ages hardly entitles you to the status of father, buddy, but I'll humor you." He gave his older brother a watered down account of his acquaintance with Page.

"Hmmm. I think you've hooked yourself into something."

"Wrong. She got to me."

"Well, hallelujah! Hope it works out. I'll be over tomorrow night instead. The full evening's yours, brother. I wouldn't take a gal I liked home at ten o'clock, not even in a small town."

Nelson exhaled sharply. "Neither would I if I hadn't wanted to accommodate you. I'll see you tomorrow evening. Thanks."

Butterflies still flitted around in his belly when he let himself remember that she'd wanted to see him badly enough to call him up and tell him so. But would she prove to be like the others? Satisfying their curiosity? Lord, he hoped and prayed she'd be different, that she'd be…He told himself to back up; she was new in town and probably wanted nothing more than friendship.

He telephoned Page precisely at six o'clock, and when she answered, her voice rested softly on his ears. "Hello."

"This is Nelson. Can you be ready at seven? I thought we'd go over to Frederick."

"Great. I don't know the customs around here. What are you wearing?"

He wondered at the question, then remembered that she came from Washington where the socially conscious were always on the ready. "A business suit. That all right?"

"Sure. People here go to dinner in jeans, and I guess I'm not used to that."

She hadn't struck him as being pretentious. Quite the contrary, but you never could tell, and he wasn't going to second guess her. "Till seven," he said, though what he wanted right then was more of her voice caressing his ears.

"B…Bye."

He had the feeling she'd wanted to say something else but dismissed it. After quickly showering and dressing, he remembered that he didn't know where she lived and called her.

"What is your address, Page?"

Her laughter rumbled to him through the wires. "I hadn't thought of that. I'm at 91-A Cochrane Drive."

He hung up and braced his hands against the wall. *Watch it, buddy. That's pure quicksand. You'd better remember who you are.*

CHAPTER THREE

Business suit, huh? She dressed in a simple sleeveless, red silk sheath that reached her knee, added pearls, pearl earrings, a pair of plain two-inch patent leather shoes and a splash of Dior's Opium. Her heart skipped a few beats when she opened her door and looked up at him. Gray suit, yellow tie and those dreamy eyes that promised paradise. He gazed down at her, liking what he saw and making no effort to hide it. After he helped her with her coat, she handed him her keys, and both his eyebrows shot up.

"What's this for?"

Had she somehow made a mistake? She'd soon know. "After you lock my door, keep them in your pocket until we get back."

He trained his gaze on her, and she battled the effect of his penetrating stare. "You aren't bringing a pocketbook? Your confidence honors me."

He took Route 144 and made it to Frederick at seven thirty-five. *He doesn't play games,* she reflected when he made none of the childish moves of some men she'd dated who used phony excuses to touch her. After the waiter seated them, she looked around at the other diners and was glad she'd dressed.

"It's lovely here," she told him. She hadn't expected such elegant fare or such a posh restaurant in that relatively small town.

He leaned forward. "So are you. I'm glad you're pleased."

Nelson leaned back in his chair, tapped his long fingers on the white linen tablecloth and cut to the chase. "I haven't gotten over your telephone call. What did it mean?"

Though surprised, his blunt honesty pleased her. She made herself look directly at him and hold his gaze while those eyes played havoc with her senses.

"It meant that I realized you weren't going to call me. I didn't know if you wanted to see me again, but I thought you might, and I…well, I…wanted to be with you again. Those few hours by the fire in your back garden were so peaceful and…and…wonderful."

If only he wouldn't look at her like that. Brown eyes ablaze with…Lord, she didn't know what. But it certainly wasn't disinterest she saw in them.

"Do you want us to see each other on a regular basis?"

Doggoned if she'd do his work for him. "If I say no, that ends it. If I say yes, I'm at a disadvantage. What do you want?"

She watched, mesmerized, as a smile played around his lips, lit up his cheek bones and then claimed his entire face. Then, to her amazement, laughter poured out of him. The first time she'd seen him laugh, really laugh.

After a minute or so, he controlled it. "I wouldn't take good money for that remark. You're a woman and a half. I want as much of your company as I can get."

She wanted to hug him. "Better not be too hasty. I've got a supply of Chuck Berry and Mahalia Jackson records right beside my Mozart and Louis Armstrong collections."

White teeth glistened against his bronze skin. "I can handle Berry and Jackson if you can stomach my Bruce Springsteen CDs."

In their delight in each other's company, they barely ate the food. He reached across the table, but before his fingers touched her hand, he stopped himself and withdrew it, and she could see him pulling back.

"You're not comfortable with our becoming…uh…better friends. Why?"

He dragged his left hand across his face, over his eyes. Then his gaze bored into her. "Comfortable? You sailed into my life like a comet streaking across a black sky. And we…uh—"

"Clicked," she supplied, since he wouldn't let himself say it.

"Yes. We clicked, and…Well, I'm trying to believe it's…that you're real."

She reached across the table and grasped his right hand. "I'm real, Nelson. If you've been alone, so have I, but I'm putting a period to that right now. What about you?"

His long, tapered fingers stroked his chin, giving the impression that he mused over her words. "You don't pull your punches, do you?"

She lifted her left shoulder in a quick shrug. "I'm tired of pretending not to be interested in a man so he can fool himself into believing he's chasing me. I'm grown, and I plan to act like it."

He sipped his coffee, savoring it to the last drop. "Why would you ever have done that?"

"In these matters, besides being a southern belle, my mother belongs to a different era, though I suspect she must have been one of the first modern women to keep her maiden name after marriage. She's brilliant, but she hardly ever touches earth. Anyway, I absorbed some of her attitudes." The thought that she was out of Millie's madcap environment warmed her and she couldn't help smiling. "I think you're interesting, so why can't I let you know it?"

"Keep talking. You'll never get rid of me."

She released his right hand. "Really? Any more tips?"

"Tips?" He winked at her. "I've got a bag full. Be sweet to me, and I'll write 'em down for you."

"Good heavens! It's almost eleven," she said after glancing at the watch that lay among the hairs at his wrist. "I had no idea it was so late. Hadn't we better go?"

He grinned at her. "Chicken. Scared of what you might do if I give you my bag of tips?" He stood and extended his hand to her.

"Don't bet on it," she said. "I'd check them out one after the other, so hand them over soon as you get the nerve."

He paid the bill and wrapped his fingers around hers as they left the restaurant. "What makes you think I don't have the nerve? I chart my own course, and no challenge or temptation has yet made me waver from it."

"First time for everything."

"Yeah? Mind if I call you tomorrow around six?"

She squeezed his fingers. "I'll mind if you don't."

On the drive back to Mystic Ridge, he didn't talk, though he glanced at her from time to time, smiled and rubbed the back of her left hand. Sweet contentment flowed out of him and enveloped her. She turned up the palm of her left hand to receive his caress.

He slowed down as they entered Mystic Ridge and paused at the red light. "I've sworn off women, Page. I've been a curio to a lot of them, a challenge. To be as tall as I am doesn't mean that I'm different from other men. I'm constructed just as they are, and I'm not immune to pain. If your goal is to conquer, forget it. I've walked over so many proverbial hot coals that my feet no longer burn. I like you a lot. I mean a lot. But I don't have to do anything about it."

She laced her fingers through his, squeezed his hand and, stunned by the fiery ripples that flashed through her, withdrew from him. "You're a sensitive man, so you recognize the difference between your past relationships and the way ours is developing. If we're going anywhere, you'll have to trust me."

The light changed, and he eased the Mercury Sable forward. "You play it close to the chest, and I don't blame you." He remained quiet for a few minutes, and she realized he was testing a thought. "My brother's spending tomorrow evening with me, and I'd like you to join us for dinner. How about it?"

"I'd like that. Is he like you?"

His short laugh surprised her. "I never thought so. Logan says whatever he thinks. And some of what he thinks can make you mad as the devil."

She blinked rapidly, wondering what would come next. "Don't you like him?"

"Logan? I love my brother. He's my closest friend. He's just a pain in the butt sometimes. You'll see." He grinned as though enjoying a private joke.

Relief coursed through her. "With that recommendation, I can hardly wait."

Nelson parked in front of her house, took her hand and walked with her to the door. Would he hold her and kiss her, banish the awful feeling that he could slip away from her like a ship easing out to the ocean? He opened her door, handed her the key and stood there looking down at her, his eyes unfathomable. She gazed up at him knowing that her eyes mirrored her expectation, her need for some semblance of intimacy with him. A kiss. A caress.

"See you tomorrow around seven," he said.

She didn't trust her voice, and her words came out in a whisper. "Okay. I'll be here."

For the longest time, he stared down at her, heat blazing in his eyes. Heat for her.

She wanted to touch him, to feel his hands on her, but she'd taken the first step, she'd called him, and she wouldn't go further. She smiled to make it easier for him, and blatant desire simmered in his eyes and proclaimed its wildness in his stance. He stepped closer, but he only stroked her cheek with gentle fingers, turned and, without a word, left her standing there.

She closed the door, walked into the darkness of her home and of her life and sat on the edge of her living room sofa. Empty. She'd needed him to hold her if only for a second. He liked her, just as he'd said, and he wanted her, but…Either he meant to take his time, or he needed some kind of assurance. She couldn't give him that. She sat up straight. What was that he'd said about his height? Oh, yes, he seemed to consider it a problem. Well, she didn't; when she looked at him, she saw a great looking man who made her think things she wouldn't mention to her mother.

Something about him drew her the way a flame lures a moth. His vulnerability? She didn't think so. His quiet calm and the peace she felt in his presence? She didn't know, but with him she felt serene, untroubled. For so long, her mother's headline-grabbing antics and the media glare that went with them had kept her life in chaos, though Millie Shipley regarded it as necessary fuel for her political career.

~⌐

"Dress casual," Nelson said when he called her the next day.

When he arrived, he looked at her long, narrow black leather skirt and jacket, red sweater blouse and low heeled black leather boots. "Well, I guess you could call that casual, but the effect certainly isn't. We're going to my place. Logan's cooking dinner." At her raised eyebrow, he added, "All right with you?"

She trusted him, didn't she? "Can he cook?"

He rolled his tongue around his right cheek and inclined his head slightly. "Oh, yes. That he can. I'd planned for us to go to Frederick for dinner and then stop by The Watering Hole to hear some good jazz."

"What changed your mind?"

"Logan. He's a good cook, so don't worry."

She slid into the front seat of his car, and he closed the door. "It doesn't occur to me to worry when I'm with you," she said.

He paused in the act of turning the key in the ignition. "Nobody's perfect, Page. I don't have a halo; I'm a man."

"Thank God for that," she murmured under her breath.

"What? Did you say what I think you said?"

She wasn't getting into that one. "How old is Logan?"

He didn't answer until he reached his house, drove through the gate and into his garage. "He's thirty-eight. He lost his family in an accident. You didn't answer my question."

His intense stare scattered her nerves, raising her temperature, and she resisted the urge to peel off her leather jacket. Annoyed at her reaction to him, she said, "You know the answer, and stop pushing me."

He cut the ignition. "What's the matter? Did I do something to upset you?"

"Yes, you did. What was wrong with kissing me good night last night? The occasion didn't call for a fifty minute clinch, so you didn't risk losing your soul. But you—"

With his hand gripping her shoulder, he turned her fully to face him. "But I…what?"

She lowered her eyelids and tried to move from his grasp, but he held her. "Open your eyes and look at me. There's something going on here, and it's nothing to play with. Are you ready for…I mean…Look! Once we get started, we're going to invest a lot of ourselves in this, and not all of it will be sweetness and bliss. You know that."

"No, I don't."

His big hand dragged her into his arms, and she stared into the dark and fierce wantonness that his eyes had become. Hunger radiated from him. Desire so fierce that she smelled it. Tasted it. Without warning, his mouth was on her hard and hot and demanding, and she opened to him as the unfamiliar softening of her heart battled the fire that raged in her loins. Closer, tighter he held her. His tongue danced wildly in her mouth until reason deserted her, and she moaned her need for relief. She sucked his tongue deeper into her mouth and tightened her grip on him, and he thrust his hand into her blouse and stroked her already beaded aureole. Her nerves rioted as he claimed her with his tongue and his stroking fingers, exhilarating her and drowning her in a pool of sensuality. And still he kneaded and stroked her while his velvet tongue plunged in and out of her. She thought she'd die if she didn't have him.

But he broke the embrace, reduced the tension and folded her gently in his arms. She couldn't speak, and when his hands cupped her face with exquisite tenderness, tears pooled in her eyes.

"I want you, and you want me, sweetheart," he whispered, "but I feel in my gut that we need to go slow. The chemistry between us is mind boggling, but I need more. Don't you?"

She buried her face in the curve of his shoulder. "There is more, at least for me," she whispered.

He stroked her cheek. "And for me. But I can't gamble with my feelings anymore. The price of losing is too high."

Her heart constricted as tendrils of fear streaked through her. "Are you saying you won't give us a chance? This is it?"

His long fingers caressed her back in soothing strokes. "Far from it. I want us to get to know each other. I want to know if the way I feel about you makes any sense, and I think we should make a serious attempt to explore this friendship."

She moved away from him and told herself to keep a lid on it. "I've got girlfriends already, Nelson. And one more thing. I don't think I said I want to have an affair with you.".

His long-lashed gaze swept over her face. Then, to her astonishment, the sound of mirth erupted from his throat, captivating her, and she thought she could listen to him laugh forever.

He rubbed the tip of her nose with his thumb. "Honey, you're a piece of work. Tell you what, soon as I'm convinced your intentions toward me are honorable, we'll get down to business."

For long minutes, she looked at him, at the twinkling devilment in his eyes, looked until a grin spread over his face. She didn't know how it happened, but they were tight in each other's arms, hugging and laughing.

"As I said before, I'm not much on mysticism, but I don't believe we met by accident. Fate had a hand in this thing or something, so let's be patient and see what's in it for us. You seeing anybody? I mean, are you committed in any way?"

She shook her head. "I don't have any ties."

"All right. Neither do I." He straightened up and reached for the door handle. "I don't know what Logan thinks we're doing out here, and I'd as soon not give him a reason to be clever. Let's go in." He locked the car and the garage door, took her hand and started for the house.

CHAPTER FOUR

"So you're Page," Logan said, the three of them standing in the doorway of the kitchen. "I can't say Nelson talked about you a lot, because he didn't, which is why I'm cooking dinner tonight. I wanted to meet you. Getting anything personal out of him is like pulling hens' teeth, and they don't have any." He grasped both of her hands. "I'm glad you agreed to come."

All she could say was, "It's a pleasure to meet you, Logan." Tall and well proportioned with a strong masculine persona and skin the color of pecan shells, he was so much like Nelson that he almost unnerved her, but she didn't flinch. He'd trained his eagle-like eyes on her, the golden rim around his brown irises accentuating the intensity of his stare. So unlike the mesmerizing sensuality of Nelson's brown eyes.

"Cut it out, Logan. You'll make her nervous. You can't decide everything about her just by looking." Nelson's arm snaked around her waist in what she recognized as a protective gesture, but she'd already decided to pull Logan down a peg if he needled her.

Logan winked at her. "I hope you like Maryland crab cakes. I got the crab meat at the Inner Harbor this afternoon." With his thumb, he motioned them out of the kitchen. "Why waste your time in here with me when you could be enjoying each other's company?"

Nelson looked at his brother, and she couldn't miss the understanding that passed between them. Two individuals attuned to each other's feelings and emotions. Nelson's expression bore nothing short of relief and, with her hand in his, he took her to the living room.

"Did I pass muster?" she asked him, though she knew the answer.

It pleased him that she cared whether his brother liked her. "What do you think?" he teased.

"I think you'd rather not say, but if I go back in there and ask him, he'll tell me."

"That, he will. Want to go cycling after church Sunday?" *Now, where had that come from?*

She nodded. "What time?"

None of the coyness he so often got from women. She grew on him with each passing second. They agreed on the time he'd pick her up and, in spite of his lectures to himself to move with care, he stepped close to her, caressed her cheek with the palm of his hand and gave her a little more of himself.

"Dinner's ready," Logan said, announcing his presence. Page shook herself back to reality and stepped away from Nelson as Logan trained his gaze on her. "Is he scared you'll disappear?"

That was a devious way of getting a confession; she had to watch it with Logan Pettiford. "Do I look that frivolous? What woman would want to escape this man?" She pointed to Nelson. *Let them digest that.*

Later, as she sipped espresso coffee, she couldn't remember having had a better meal. "You're some cook."

"Glad you enjoyed it. Tell me, what's a sophisticated woman like you doing out here in the boondocks? Running away from anything?"

Nelson's antennae shot up. He'd wondered about that, but had decided it might be too soon to question her, since he had a string of things he wasn't ready to share with her.

"I'm not running," he heard her say. "I'm looking—for myself, for my independence and…" something else, she thought suddenly. "I want to stretch myself to my limits."

"And you think you'll find all of that here?"

Nelson intervened. He wouldn't let Logan, an accomplished attorney, interrogate her. "Ease up, Logan. Aren't her reasons for being here the same as mine?"

"All right, man, but you know me." He winked at Page. "Stick with him. No matter how it looks, he's worth it."

Nelson stood. "It's time I took you home." He pointed to Logan. "When that philosopher's got his belly full and a snifter of good cognac in his hands, he's ready to roll." Logan walked with them to the door and, to Nelson's amazement, embraced Page.

"That's a first," Nelson told her, standing with her at her front door. "Logan is not a demonstrative man. I'll be out of town tomorrow, but I'll be at your place Sunday at one. Okay?" Unwilling either to draw them into heated passion or to leave without kissing her, he looked down at her willing lips, brushed them with his own and turned away.

"Now, who's chicken?" she called after him.

"Me. I freely admit it. See you Sunday." Her laughter wrapped around him, warming his heart as he headed home.

How could she know what it meant to him to have a woman who attracted him as she did behave as if his height was not unusual? A woman who didn't comment on the obvious and who seemed to accept what she saw of him. A woman who, with her intelligence, had to know about Nelson Pettiford, the writer; and with what she'd seen of his lifestyle, she had to know he was that man. Either she liked him for himself or she was someone special in her own right and unfazed by celebrity. Whichever, he liked the result. If their relationship continued to progress, he'd know it all, but he believed in biding his time.

He'd meant to go straight to bed, get up early and sketch some cartoons, but his entire system seemed charged, an engine revved and ready to go. He knew he wouldn't sleep, so he went into his den and started work on a cartoon. He sketched several but couldn't bring Quigley to life. Finally, with Odessa-Cat frolicking beside him, the big tom prowled along Old Mills Road complaining about human beings.

"Only an idiot would think of putting street lights on this road. What do people think moonlight's for?" Quigley said to Odessa-Cat.

"Don't ask me," Odessa-Cat said. "I long since forgot what moonlight-light's for."

Quigley slanted his gray eyes in her direction. "You had your day, girl, and I sure enjoyed you."

Suddenly, Quigley stopped walking. "I always get an eerie feeling out here on Old Mills Road, but I still can't seem to stay away from here. Let's go back."

Odessa-Cat rubbed herself against Quigley, but the wily tomcat merely stretched lazily and licked his chops. "Ain't no point in sidling up to me, girl. Come on."

Nelson stared at his creation, nonplussed as to where the idea had come from. Musing over it, he realized that he often got an eerie feeling on that very same road, but he loved to drive along it at sunset, when the multi-hued rays of the dying sun enthralled him and made him feel alive. Funny, that it was there he had met Page. Hmmm.

Page kicked off her shoes, put on her stack of Louis Armstrong CDs and danced herself into exhaustion. What was the matter with her? In all her twenty-nine years, never before had a man kicked her libido into perpetual overdrive. She ought to be suspicious of the whole thing, but he was so sweet, and being with him exhilarated her. She thought back to earlier that evening with him and his brother. Logan liked her and encouraged her relationship with Nelson. They saw something admirable in her, wanted her friendship, and they weren't trying through her to get anything from Millie Shipley, weren't courting her mother for favors.

She went to the phone and called her mother's private number. She didn't telephone her mother often, because just talking with Millie wore her out.

"Darling," Millie began as soon as she said hello, "I was going to call you, but this town is one living cyclone. Congressman Boney is going to get a piece of my mind. You just wait. Oh, yes. We're going to the White House Tuesday after next for the reception preceding the Kennedy Center Honors. So get a new formal. Not pink. That's what I'm wearing. Mary Jasper is on the honors list. What for, I don't know, but they always have to have at least one African American out of the five. When are you coming home? Call me to make sure I'm here. You know—"

Page took a deep breath and broke into Millie's torrent of words. "Mama, I'm not going to that reception. So get somebody else to go with you. I'll let you know when I can get over to Washington. The job is—"

"All right, honey. My other line is flashing. Mother loves you. Bye."

Page fell back on the bed. "How'd I ever stand the stress of living in the house with her?" she said aloud. "Much as I love her, I sure am glad I left there."

Sunday afternoon, she dressed warmly in down pants and jacket, got her headgear and waited for Nelson's one-one-three-one ring. She opened the door and laughed when she saw that he'd chosen down pants and jacket the same shade of blue as her own. His quick kiss didn't satisfy her, but she knew that was all she'd get right then. He took her bike from her and stored it with his own on the rack over his bumper.

"Where're we going?"

"Stone Mountain Park, about forty minutes from here. The trails are fantastic. I've always biked over there by myself, but it's so peaceful, so quiet and so…so beautiful that…Well, at least today I'll be able to enjoy it with someone…with you."

He'd been lonely, she surmised, maybe even lonelier than she, who had hungered for meaningful friendships to replace the superficial relationships she experienced in the rarefied atmosphere of her famous mother's orbit.

"I'm…I'm glad my car stalled out on Old Mills Road and that you happened along."

He didn't look at her, but she knew from the way his jaw worked that he was dealing with an emotion she'd stirred in him. He reached over and laid his right hand on her left one.

"I told you once that I didn't believe in things I couldn't understand. Like Fate. But I'm not so sure now. The evening we met, I turned into that road by mistake because my thoughts weren't on my driving. I was sure I'd already passed Old Mills Road. Fate? I just don't know."

In the park, they cycled for almost an hour, not speaking, enjoying the beauty of autumn's last gasp. Then, he guided them back to the car. "I brought some snacks if you'd like something." They sat on an old stone bench beneath the trees that seemed to reach the sky, while the evening sun hovered closer and closer to its place of rest. "You can have ham, smoked salmon and chicken sandwiches, and I've got a thermos of coffee and some ginger ale, since you don't drink colas."

She looked up at him, saw the concern for her comfort reflected in his face and in his whole demeanor and asked herself how she'd gotten so lucky. She told him she'd start with the chicken sandwich and coffee. He poured a cup of coffee for her and added milk. So he'd noticed that she didn't add sugar. Taking it from him, she smiled as best she could, because if she cried…

"Want some grapes?" he asked after she'd eaten three sandwiches.

She nodded, and he picked one from the cluster and held it to her mouth. Her lips accepted it and the next and the next until she made herself look into eyes that shimmered with a sweet something that wrung a gasp from her throat. In spite of her vow of prudence, she reached for him; she couldn't help it, and in a split second, he had her in his arms. Holding her. Stroking her. Wanting to feel his mouth on her, she kissed his cheek and, when he looked at her, she claimed him. He slipped his tongue between her parted lips, but only for a second and then hugged her to him. Every molecule of her body warmed to his cherishing, his gentle loving.

Her heart told her that he'd seeped deep into her, that because of him, she knew what she'd missed and what she needed and that if they walked away from each other, she'd never be the same. Now's the time to tell him who you are, her conscience advised, but she couldn't risk dragging her mother's fame into their relationship. She'd better tell him about her work, though, because she didn't want him to suspect her of using him.

With her hand still in his, she shifted her body to face him. "Before we go any further, I'd better tell you something."

She sensed his tension in the hand she held, and his defensiveness mirrored itself in his eyes like a swordsman *en garde*.

"What is it?"

"I'm a journalist, and I work for *The Mystic Ridge Observer.*"

He stared at her and eased his fingers out of her hand. "Are you kidding me?"

She shook her head. "That's what I do, but I will never write one word about you. Never! When I asked my boss where you lived and told him why I wanted to find you, he gave me your address and asked me to interview you. But after those precious hours I spent with you that afternoon, no one could have paid me to invade your privacy. When I got to work that next Monday morning, I told him you refused to see me."

The fingers of his right hand moved back and forth across his chin, and while she waited for his response, tiny needles pierced every nerve in her body.

"I see."

"D…don't you believe me?"

"I do believe you. It's been almost two months, so you've had opportunities to write about me. But I read that paper, and I haven't seen your byline. How's that?"

"My column's in the features section under the name, Twice Shy."

"I know the people in Mystic Ridge are curious about me, and I know they've imagined all kinds of things about me. I'm also certain you've heard a lot of it. Rodgers has too, and when he discovers we're friends—and small towns being what they are, he certainly will—he'll pressure you. Then what?"

"It won't be the first time I've changed jobs."

He nodded. "That's the only paper in Mystic Ridge. You'd have to leave here."

"I'm not going to write a story on you. Period."

His gaze lingered on her. And then, as though having arrived at an important conclusion, he leaned back against the bench. "I'll be in Washington Tuesday night and Wednesday morning. Can we be together Wednesday evening?"

Her heartbeat returned to normal and she let herself smile. "I'm already looking forward to it."

After emptying their refuse in the wire basket that rested beside an elm, he walked back and took her hand. "It gets dark earlier and earlier these days. I think we ought to head back to Mystic."

He drove slowly over the two-lane highway that wound its way between trees that seemed to touch the sky, the last of their leaves fluttering gracefully to the earth. The only words that came to her mind were those that said peace, contentment, paradise.

"Do you think we can do this again before it gets too cold?" he asked.

She nodded. "I love the outdoors and especially the water. Next time, let's ride around the lake. We can go anytime; just whistle."

"Yeah? If I did that, you'd think I'd lost my mind."

He braked quickly, and his right arm shot out as though to protect her. A smile had taken possession of his face, and she glanced at the highway in front of them expecting to see a deer or a bear. But strolling casually across the paved road were a goose and her five little goslings.

"Nature's wonderful," he said, when the birds disappeared into the underbrush.

What a sweet man, she thought, then folded her arms and settled back into the comfort of the aura that his presence wrapped around her. James Rodgers could beg all he pleased; he'd never get a story about Nelson Pettiford out of her.

CHAPTER FIVE

Nelson flexed his shoulders to get used to the cut of the tux he hadn't worn in nearly a year, stepped out of the Willard Hotel and into a Capital Cab. "The White House, please."

"You got a pass, buddy? I ain't gittin' in that long line for nothin'."

He showed the driver the pass and, fifteen minutes later, stepped out of the taxi and into the White House. He'd had his jacket tailored with an extra inside pocket so he'd have places to keep his little note pads as well as his miniature recorder. His status as best-selling author thrice over got him more invitations than he bothered to accept, but he wasn't so blasé or jaded as to turn down a White House reception for the Kennedy Center Honorees. The President surprised him with the comment that he'd read and liked his last book; he thought the First Lady warmer and more feminine than her press and pictures suggested.

He ordered a wine glass of ginger ale with ice and mingled. He'd thought Art Buchwald taller, and Brokaw didn't look nearly his age.

Congresswoman Dr. Millie Shipley held court with three first-year congressmen and one old pro whose demeanor suggested an interest in more than her words.

Her eyes reminded him of someone; he couldn't figure out who, but he didn't give much thought to it. He spied two senators in heated discussion and inched close enough to discern that Senator Painter wanted the health care bill floored and Ballard swore it wouldn't happen. Power. Power. The entertainment at the Kennedy Center proved uninspired; he thought the honorees deserved better. The applause had hardly ceased before he was back in the Willard Hotel.

He ate a light supper in his room and listened to his recorded notes. He sketched Quigley snarling at a tomcat that had invaded his territory.

"There's room enough here for both of us," the intruder said.

"But my space is germ free, Brother Tom," Quigley said, "and the way you chase these little hot trollops, you're full of disease. Stay out. I don't have any health insurance."

Brother Tom stuck his tail between his legs, his face, a caricature of Congressman Ballard, glum and arrogant. "Ain't no way you can stay healthy, Quigley, if my little hot trollops are full of disease. No amount of insurance will save you, so forget that."

"That's how you feel about all the poor cats in this country," Quigley said, raising his head and prancing off. "Later for you, Brother Tom."

Satisfied with the piece, he reached for the phone and dialed Page's number. "This is Nelson, I hope you hadn't gone to bed."

"No. I was editing my story."

He marveled that they had so much in common, but he couldn't tell her about that. Not yet. "Remember our date tomorrow? If you like, we could drive over to Baltimore. The choice is between an African American Arts Show, The Soloisti di Zagreb with a program of Mozart chamber music and the Preservation Hall Jazz Band. If we leave early, we can take in the art show and one of the other two. What's your pleasure?"

"Whatever you can get tickets for. Just tell me what to wear and what time to be ready."

She never pretended, never fuzzed an issue. "I'll call you as soon as I have something definite."

"You can call me before then."

He rolled over in the bed and lay flat on his back. "Is that so? You aren't playing with me, are you?"

The silence lasted a little longer than he'd anticipated. "Uh...no. Well, not really. I mean, I may be teasing, but I mean it."

"What kind of double talk is that?" He fell over on his belly, ready to test her mettle. "I mean business."

Her giggle reached him through the wires, soothing him and exciting him as well. She said, "Me too."

A grin crawled over his face, and he waited, certain that she'd back down. "No kidding. You write a great score, baby," he said when she didn't, "but I want to hear you sing the tune."

He could imagine that her eyes widened as they did when she got a surprise.

"Soprano or mezzo? I've got a wide range, and I'm no stranger to the scales."

"How often do you practice?" he asked, warming up to the game.

She cleared her throat. "That's the problem. I don't remember when I last practiced. I must be kind of rusty."

How much truth was in that jostling? He propped himself up on his elbows, more serious now. "A serious musician rehearses regularly."

"Is that what we're talking about? Music? I must have gotten lost somewhere."

"Be careful, Page," he growled. "I can be in Mystic Ridge in an hour and a half."

"But I wouldn't want you to get jacked up for speeding or maybe get in an accident."

"Why don't you just say 'uncle'? You're chicken and you're backing down."

"Am not. If you want to come all the way here just to kiss me good night, I wouldn't think of objecting."

He held the phone away and stared at it. Whether she knew it or not, she was definitely kidding.

"You still there?" she asked.

"Yeah, but you give me one reason, and I'll be out of here in fifteen minutes."

"What's here for you will wait till tomorrow, and you can get a good night's sleep and drive refreshed in the morning."

"What's there for me, Page?" Maybe he ought to stop before he said more than he intended, but right then all he could think of was the heat of her body when he touched her and the hunger that racked his loins. Hunger for her alone.

"You told me to be careful; I'm giving you the same advice," she said. "You're not ready to know where I stand, but if you urge me the tiniest bit, I'll tell you. Can I have a kiss?"

"Can you have...open your mouth, baby."

Arousal slammed into him, and his breath came in short gasps. What the hell had he done to himself? Get it together, man.

"Good night." He whispered it lest she detect his total disarray.

"Good night, love." She hung up, and he lay there. Unstrung.

Nelson hadn't reached the point of commitment, and he'd intimated that he wanted to be prudent and let them care for and understand each other before they became intimate. She knew he didn't intend to have a casual affair, and if he decided he wasn't in it for the long haul, she doubted he'd let her get any closer to him. That suited her perfectly, and it told her more about him than he could explain with words.

But tonight, he'd come close to breaching the bounds he set for himself, and it behooved her not to play with him. If she caused him to violate his own standards, he might hold it against her.

The next morning, she dressed in a burnt orange-colored woolen suit, a beige blouse and brown shoes and accessories. She wasn't overdressed, but she figured she could go wherever he took her that evening.

"Hey, girl, you really hung it on this morning," Phyllis said. "Who is he?"

Page let her have a slow burn. "I dress to please myself, and my mood this morning said burnt orange. Since this is the only thing I own in this color, this is what I'm wearing."

"Well, go out and buy a slew of stuff that color."

"Yeah, it suits you." She turned around to see James Rodgers, her boss, standing in the doorway.

How does he know what color I'm wearing? she wanted to ask him. He'd glued his gaze on Phyllis, his copy editor. The phone rang and she reached for it, but Phyllis grabbed it first.

"*Observer.* How may I help you?" She listened for a second. "Uh…she's right here."

Page took the phone, covered the mouthpiece with her hand and said, "Let that be the last time you answer my phone when I'm sitting here, unless I ask you to do it."

"Well kiss my grits."

Page turned her back to them. "Hello."

"Hi. This is Nelson."

"I know. What did you find out?"

"That's not the greeting I expected. You got company?"

"Yes. Sorry. I'll make up for it."

"I'll pick you up at four-thirty. Office or home?"

"I'll be at the office," she told him.

"I'll call you around one. Okay?"

"Right. Kiss me, and make it good."

"You'll be sorry for that one. Talk with you later."

She hung up, turned and it didn't surprise her that she had the attention of both James and Phyllis. A couple of sharp comments came to mind, but she swallowed them.

"Can I do something for either one of you?" she asked, instead.

Phyllis shrugged. "You been here a couple of months, and you're already whispering to some guy on the phone. Way to go, girl."

Page chose not to comment, finished retyping her column and took it across the hall to the features editor. "Is it good?" he asked her.

"Flawless," she said and headed for the elevator. She wanted to talk with Nelson, and she didn't want to wait another hour and a half. She called him from a phone booth in the building's lobby. After the fifth ring, she heard his voice on the answering machine. Deep and soothing.

"This is Page, I—"

"What a surprise! I'm glad you called. Our earlier conversation left me dissatisfied and wanting more. Much more."

"I suspect those busybodies will be watching to see whether anyone meets me this evening. I'll be proud to have you come to my office for me. It's your call."

"In that case, I'll be at your office at four-thirty."

"I'm in room four-sixteen. Turn left at the top of the stairs."

"Are you sure, babe?"

"I've never been more positive of anything. See you at four-thirty."

She saw no reason why they shouldn't see each other when and wherever they wished. They were both single. The good citizens of Mystic Ridge may have peculiar notions about him, but she knew how wrong they were, and if being seen with him would change their minds, she was more than happy to walk hand-in-hand with him.

"But you'll have to wait for your kiss; I don't think I should do that in my office."

His laughter caressed her ears, and she suspected not for the first time that, if he let her, she could love him. *Yes, if he'll let you,* her mind challenged.

Nelson hung up, braced his elbows on his drafting board and gave in to his emotions as tremor after tremor slashed through his body. A companion, a woman who enjoyed his company, who wanted her colleagues to know that he was important to her and who asked nothing of him other than his friendship. A woman who, in two months, hadn't alluded to his status as a celebrity author and who had never mentioned his height of nearly seven feet. Had he finally found a woman to love, to care for and who would cherish him above all others? He went to the refrigerator and got a glass of orange juice in the hope that the potassium would slow his heartbeat. After a few minutes, he sat down to put the finishing touches on the cartoon he'd begun the night before in the hotel. He gave Quigley an added bit of tabby hair in the forehead and signed it Slim Wisdom as he always did.

Nelson prepared himself for the astonishment that Page's colleagues would exhibit when they saw him, and he appreciated Page's efforts to forestall that, though he didn't need their approval nor their good manners.

The door stood ajar, and when he entered, the sweet woman rounded her desk immediately, took his hand and reached up to him with her face upturned. Thinking she wanted to tell him something, he leaned down and, to his amazement, she kissed his cheek.

"Phyllis, this is Nelson."

"Hi. Well, hi. I have to say I never expected to meet you."

"Hello, Phyllis," he said, with amusement. "I'm glad to know you." Just for the hell of it, he winked at her. "Was it you who answered the phone when I called this morning?"

Phyllis swallowed hard. "That was you?"

He looked down at Page. "Was it?"

He felt her fingers tug at his hand. "You know it was, and stop pulling her leg."

He helped Page into her coat and, for reasons he didn't guess at, put his arm around her. As if to reward him for the audacious act, she let a brilliant smile light up her face and warmth suffused him.

"We'd better be going. Nice meeting you, Phyllis."

"Sure thing, Nelson," Phyllis said, and he could see that she was practically in a stupor.

"See you in the morning," Page called to her colleague over her shoulder.

"Why'd you kiss me on the cheek in your office?" he asked as they sped toward Baltimore.

"Just spreading the word that you are not available. By noon tomorrow, this town will know that you and I are seeing each other, and you'll have to step around the women."

He slowed down to seventy. "You couldn't be serious. They've left me alone for eighteen months."

Her laughter was gentle, yet invigorating like a rustling spring breeze. "You ever heard of royal tasters? They tasted the food before the sovereign ate it to make sure it wasn't poisoned. You could say these women will regard me as a tester, if not taster."

Lord, it felt good to laugh, and he let himself enjoy it. "You're pure joy. I'm already forgetting what my life was like before you walked into it."

From the moment they stepped into the art gallery, she appeared captivated by the paintings, most of which were abstracts, and he had to bide his time until they reached the drawings.

She commented on his preference for them. "You seem more interested in the drawings than in the paintings. I like the drawings, but I'm not sure I understand what the artist is saying. I love paintings."

"I love both," he said. Better not get into a discussion of their relative merits; he might give himself away. That thought brought to mind another issue that he'd better do something about. He hadn't told her he was Nelson Pettiford the author, though he suspected that with her sophistication, she knew. But if she didn't, he'd rather she didn't learn it through the media.

A group of Romare Bearden drawings caught his eye. So many black artists painted with great power and, yet, with so much less recognition than they deserved. He stood before the man's work, admiring the craftsmanship and inventiveness until her fingers slipped through his, warm and tender.

"You really like these, don't you? I've never paid much attention to them. Maybe you'll explain them to me sometime so I'll know what to look for."

He heard her words, but had no idea what she'd said. His mind, his whole being had focused on her

smile, on the evidence that she knew she had the right
to take his hand and hold it.

"What's the matter?"

He'd been staring at her. But how could he not? A
woman who seemed to fit him perfectly. At times,
he'd swear he was deep in a dream.

"I know you're real," he said, "but sometimes I
don't see how you could be."

"You mean because we like the same things?"

He shook his head. "That too. But everything
about you appeals to me. At my age, I never expected
to meet a woman who would touch me as you have
and who would…well…" He couldn't finish because
he wasn't that sure, didn't know what he was to her.

"And who would enjoy being with you
and…and—"

"And what, Page?" The urgency in his voice
shocked him as his words flew out to her on wings of
prayer.

She didn't hesitate, nor did she take her eyes from
his gaze. "And who thinks you're the most wonderful
man she's ever met."

As though of their own accord, both of his hands
grasped her shoulders, and he stared down at her
knowing his eyes mirrored what was in his heart.
"There's so much you don't know. I haven't felt alone
since I've known you. Don't encourage me unless
you're serious, unless you mean what you say. You're a
lovely woman, and you don't have to take second best.

Unless you care for me, I need to put on the brakes right this minute."

She looked up at him, her face open and vulnerable. "You don't care more for me than I care for you. If you put on the brakes, as you termed it, I'll have to do the same. I understand what you're telling me, but the citizens of Mystic Ridge are foolish." Suddenly, she grinned. "Imagine, I can go out and buy a slew of spiked-heel shoes and, even if that puts me over six feet, it won't matter."

"You say all that in here in the presence of all these people when I can't…" His pounding heart sent his blood speeding through his body as the force and meaning of her words planted themselves in his brain. This wasn't the time to explore with her what he felt and needed, not there in that crowded gallery. He glanced at his watch.

"We'd better get something to eat. The concert begins at eight."

While they walked to his car, he took her hand in his and tucked them both in his coat pocket. Gusts of wind pelted his face as they strode along, and he wanted to shield her from the stinging air. But with her face up and head back, she seemed to glory in it. In the car at last, he locked the doors and reached across her to buckle her seat belt. He knew she could do it, but it pleased him to buckle it for her.

She leaned back against the headrest and treated him to a smile that shot pinions of desire straight through him.

"You can kiss me now." She wet her lips, parted them and raised her long-lashed gaze in an electrifying invitation. He'd have taken her to his body even if there had been a trap door beneath his feet. At the touch of his tongue against her lips, she pulled him into her and loved him as if she'd been starved for his touch, his taste, as if she couldn't get enough of him. Her fingers caressed his nape, and he tightened his hold on her. Moans erupted from her throat, exciting and thrilling him, and in his deceptive mind he had her beneath his naked body thrashing and undulating against him. He had to brake it or he'd lose control, had to stop the sweet and awful fire she'd built in his loins. But she let herself go, sucking on his tongue as if it were the essence of her life. *Stop it, man.* But it felt so good and for so long, all of his life, he'd needed the loving she gave him.

He had to…With all the control he could muster, he pushed himself away.

She stared up at him, as if trying to see through a fog. "What…what is it?"

He let his hand brush her cheek in the only intimacy he dared permit himself. "Honey, you had me close to the point of explosion. I'm…I'm anything but hungry for food right now, but we…" He cleared his throat. *Get it together, man.* "We have to eat." She continued to gaze at him, the picture of innocence. He shook his head in bemusement. "Baby, you're lethal." He turned the key in the ignition and prayed he could keep his mind on his driving.

CHAPTER SIX

At the Crystal Cove Restaurant, they took their seats in a booth facing the Baltimore Bay. Reflections of lights from the Inner Harbor danced across Nelson's face. His precious face, Page thought, and acknowledged to herself that he was the man she wanted. Their explosive passion minutes earlier had taken her appetite, at least for food, so she ordered a poached filet of sole, the least filling entree on the menu.

"I think I'll have the same," Nelson said, and she didn't miss his lack of enthusiasm for it.

They finished the meal, and he moved around and sat beside her in the booth. "Maybe I should have told you this earlier, but I didn't. Anyhow, I suspect you may already know that I'm the same Nelson Pettiford who wrote three novels that made the *New York Times* list. I didn't mention it, because I wanted you to like me for myself."

She didn't need his confession, but it pleased her that he trusted her enough to tell her. "You're right; I knew it, and I liked the fact that you didn't try to impress me. Nothing would have sent me running from you faster. I've had my fill of that. That night on Old Mills Road, you told me that if I wouldn't let you take me into town, you'd park on the other side of the road from me and stay there all night to make certain no one bothered me. I wouldn't have been more impressed with you if you had won a Nobel prize."

He stared at her so long that tension gathered in her, and a restlessness suffused her. As though realizing that he unsettled her, he squeezed her fingers in reassurance, but that exacerbated the damage, and desire shot through her like a twister. His right arm brought her to him, and he patted her shoulder. But she wasn't fooled; he needed to touch her, and a pat was all he risked right then.

Three hours later they walked out of the concert hall and into the biting, early-December wind. "It'll probably be too cold to bike," he said, his voice tinged with regret, "but we could drive over to the Monocacy River, fish and cook the catch on the river bank. We could build a nice fire. Want to?"

She did, though she'd never had a fishing pole in her hands. For the remainder of that week and on the weekend, they explored Mystic Ridge and its environs, fishing in Monocacy River, walking in Stone Mountain Park and cycling through nearby woods and alongside Lake Linganore. For the first time, she had a companion, and she told him in many little ways that he had a special place in her life.

The following Monday morning, Page met Mr. Whitfield as he strode up with the mail. He tipped his hat and took the mail from his sack.

"Young lady, you've set this town on its head. At every stop I make, people are asking me about Pettiford. They're not sure they've read him right because if they had, a sane woman like you wouldn't be walking around holding hands with him. Unless there's something special about you, too." He chuckled. "You watch out when the sistahs realize they passed on the real thing."

She felt good. For two cents, she'd spread her wings and fly. "Serves them right. Every one of them," she said. "They isolated him, treated him as if he weren't human. But he is, and he's wonderful."

"I won't ask how you happened to figure that out, but I tip my hat to you. He's a fine man. Solid as they come."

No sooner had she walked into her office and sat at her desk than her boss appeared at the door. "I'd say you're a fast worker. "

She remembered Mr. Whitfield's words, and a cold dampness settled around her neck and on her forehead. Here it comes, she thought, and braced herself for the worst.

"I want a story on Pettiford for the next issue. It'll go right on the front page under your real name. A sell-out. Can you get me a picture of him, preferably with you or somebody standing right beside him?"

Anger furled up in her, and she told herself not to lose her temper. "So you noticed we're friends, and you want me to do a story on him to appease the curiosity of people who've shunned him for the eighteen months he's been here? If you wanted a story on him, why didn't you call him, invite him to lunch and interview him? Sorry!"

Incredulity masked his face. "You're saying you won't do it?"

She unlocked her computer. "You got it. We're friends, James, and I don't intend for him to think I've developed a friendship with him in order to get a story."

He walked to her desk, and she could see that he didn't believe she'd said it. "You're a reporter, and I'm only telling you to do your job. He was here, and he knows you work for a newspaper."

From his stance, she didn't expect to win, but she made one last appeal. "I care for him, James, and he's given me his trust. I won't betray him, not for this job or anything else. If you wish, I'll give you my resignation."

He stared at her. "You don't know a thing about that guy, and yet you'd ditch your job for him?"

She released a long, tired breath. "You're the one who doesn't know anything about him. You and these people who call him weird, crazy, dangerous, an outlaw and a lot of other things that would hurt him if he knew. If you want me to leave, just say so."

His shoulders sagged. "I won't ask you to leave, but you've just ruined your chance to report hard news, and I'm dropping your column. Go down to the senior center and find out if anything's going on there that would interest anybody."

"But—"

"You asked for it. Take it or leave it." With that he turned on his heels and stomped away.

"I'm sorry," Phyllis said. "I wish I hadn't mentioned it to him. But he was so happy when he figured he'd finally get that story. Maybe if I talk to him—"

"It's all right, Phyllis. I'm a good reporter, and I know it. When I get tired of visiting with the seniors, I'll move on." She consoled herself with the thought that it ought to be more fun working in Frederick.

"I didn't see your byline in the paper this week," Nelson said to her several evenings later as they sat in her kitchen making pecan pralines. "What happened? You missed your deadline?"

"Naaah," she said, as if the matter were of no importance. "I'm checking out the seniors at the center on Boyers Mill Road. Fascinating." She hadn't meant to sound sarcastic, but nearly a week of boredom had that effect.

"You mean…Wait a minute. Back up. You've been demoted. That's what this is about, isn't it?"

"It's nothing," she hedged. "I got a new assignment is all."

He stopped placing pecans in the middle of the candies and got up from the table. "Did he ask you to write a story about me?" When she didn't answer and wouldn't look at him, he persisted. "Did he? I'll hound you till you tell me the whole story."

She let the air out of her lungs. "Okay, so he asked me. I told him I wouldn't do it." She related the remainder of it while he paced from one end of the kitchen to the other and back.

"He can't do this to you. I'll give you the interview. Carte blanche. Ask me anything."

She had expected he'd react this way. "Please stop pacing, and sit down before this stuff gets hard. I am not, repeat not, going to write a story on you for this newspaper or any other. Period. I told you that, and I'm good as my word. Besides, I refuse to satisfy the curiosity of the gossip-mongers in this town. And that's final."

"Well—"

She wasn't sure she was ready for what the expression on his face implied. "Well what?"

"Is it just a matter of keeping your word, or do you care this much for me?"

She stiffened. Until he told her how he felt about her, she'd let him figure it out from her behavior. Besides, she wasn't jumping over that bridge before she got to it.

"I care about you," she said, fumbling her way. "You're old enough to figure out things yourself."

The smile nearly made it to his eyes. Eyes that made her think and feel things she couldn't share with a living soul. He needed to know where he stood; she knew that, but he'd have to give a little.

He lifted his right shoulder in a light shrug. "I know you light up like a furnace when I touch you and that you care about me. Yes." He trained his mesmeric gaze on her for a long minute. "But you've given me something I never had, and—"

She scrambled from the table, stood and faced him. "You wanted to take it slow. Well so do I. That doesn't mean you aren't important to me, because you are—"

Warm and eager, his mouth covered her own, and his hands held her to him, his caress gentle. The touch of his fingers stroking her hair, her cheeks and her shoulder in feather-soft touches bound her to him with the strength of ancient chains. His lips adored her eyes, the tip of her nose and her chin, swathing her in the bittersweet agony of love. Tremors rippled through her, as he cherished her, and she locked her arms around his waist. Not the mind-blowing passion into which he'd always drawn her, but a sweet and exquisite caring. He folded her to him and tucked her head to his breast, and her tears of happiness soaked his shirt.

"I think I'd better go now."

Torn between her head and her emotions, she hugged him. "You make me so happy."

She could see that he forced the smile. "I'm happy too, but it's best I leave. Make no mistake, Page, one of these nights I won't leave you unless you tell me to go. Is that clear?"

She nodded. He kissed her quickly and left, but if he had wanted to stay…She let the thought hang. *Your days are numbered, girl,* she said to herself as she closed the door behind him.

Nelson walked into his house and sat down to gather his thoughts. Maybe he shouldn't have left Page, but she had become a part of him, had buried herself into his every sinew, every molecule of his body from his feet to his scalp. Yet, they didn't know each other. Hell, he didn't even know her birthday, the names of her parents or where she was born. As much as they talked, and they talked all the time, they hadn't talked enough about themselves. He intended to correct that, because he was leaning toward the point of no return. His gaze landed on *The Washington Post*. He scrutinized an item in the lower left-hand corner, turned to page nineteen and read the remainder. With the paper in hand, he went to his drafting board. Millie Shipley was visiting local African American beauty parlors in support of small businesses, and she'd already had her hair done at three of them that day. When asked whether she planned to charge the government for her hairdos, she had replied, "It's part of the job, at least for today." Partly amused and partly vexed, he began his cartoon.

"Where you going tonight, Quigley?" Odessa-Cat asked.

"Staying home, Odessa-Cat. At thirty dollars for a hair trim, I can't afford to leave this alley. Where you going?"

"I found an expense account voucher for the House of Representatives that somebody lost, so I guess that ought to take care of things. I'm gonna have a night on the town."

"You're not scared you'll get into trouble with taxpayer advocate Millie-Cat? You know how she rages about every little thing."

"No problem," Odessa-Cat said. "Millie-Cat's getting her hair done at every beauty parlor in Washington and charging it to the government. She can't raise the devil about me this time."

Quigley licked his fur. "She should be glad she's not representing me. I'd picket her on Capitol Hill."

He sketched Millie-Cat's face to resemble Millie Shipley and signed it Slim Wisdom.

The phone rang, and he hoped he'd hear Page's voice. "How's it going, brother? You sound disappointed. How're things with you and Page?"

He settled back for a long talk with Logan. "Page is fine. How's it going with you?" He didn't want to talk about her, not even with his brother, so he changed the subject. "A while back, I set up a foundation to help children, and I've decided to help the kids who suffer because they're different, as I have. Living in this conservative town has made me more aware than ever of what it means to stand out."

They discussed Nelson's plans for his foundation a bit more, then turned the talk to the case Logan was trying in civil court, but Nelson's heart wasn't in the conversation and their talk soon ended. He wanted to speak with Page, to tell her everything about himself, though he didn't consider that prudent at the time. He'd never doubted himself before, but he'd never loved a woman, either.

In the library several days later, he noticed a group of children who were returning some books and checking out others. Two boys and a girl were severely deformed and one boy spoke with difficulty. All were well behaved for their age, around five or six.

"Who are those children?" Nelson asked a boy who was shelving books.

"They're from the group home."

A little girl with sad eyes covered the left side of her face with her hand when she caught him looking at her, and his heart turned over when he saw the mark she tried to hide. She signed for her book and walked past him with her head turned away from him. The next day, he went to the group home where he learned that all the children there had been abandoned, and he vowed to help as much as he could.

"What are you telling me?" he asked Page several evenings later when they spoke by phone.

"The Ridgeway Senior Center is not the dullest place in Mystic Ridge. A Mrs. Cook claimed that she always missed money out of her pocket book when she came back from lunch. It seems they are encouraged to leave their belongings in their little lockers. I then discovered that over half the seniors I spoke with there last Tuesday complained about the same thing," Page said with a ring of excitement in her voice. "They're afraid to tell the management, because the center is their whole life. It's that or stay home alone. If that weren't enough, I find that some of the workers borrow money from the seniors and don't repay it. We're speaking fifty, a hundred and more at a time. James Rodgers thought he was punishing me, but he may have done me a favor."

"If I were you, I'd keep it under my hat till I was ready to hand it in."

She told him she planned doing volunteer work at the senior center. He thought for a minute. "Unless you must be at that center, I've got a suggestion."

He told her that a year earlier he'd established a foundation to help children who weren't physically handicapped but who, like him, had traits that made them different.

"I need to publicize it, but I haven't been able to do that here and remain anonymous. Whether it's counselling they need, surgery, whatever. I know what it's like, and I want to help."

Her voice floated to him like music. "That's wonderful. I'll get a notice in the paper. Since it's charity, it won't cost anything."

"Great," he said. "How about a movie tomorrow night? Robert De Niro. There's a Danny Glover, too, but I've seen it."

He imagined that she grinned because he knew she loved De Nero. "Say no more. What time?"

"Five thirty. Let's eat dinner after the movie." She told him goodbye.

"Hey," he yelled. "What about my kiss?"

"Well, you didn't ask."

"I didn't ask? Since when did I have to ask?"

"I like to know you want it."

"You like to…" He got up and walked as far as the phone line would permit. "Page, are you trying to send me to an insane asylum? Well, lady, let me tell you I want that and more." He lowered his voice and spoke in soft tones. "I want you, Page, in every way that a man can want a woman. I thought you knew that, but if you don't, I plan to remind you often. Very often. Got that?"

She laughed, and he wished he'd been looking at her so he could figure out what that laugh meant. "You make it sound like a punishment," she said. "I thought I was getting something super special, but—"

"I realize you like to challenge me sometimes, but could we just skip that right now? I want a kiss, and if you can't manage it over the phone the way you usually do, I'm coming over there."

"I'll meet you at my front door, but you can't stay."

"I'll be right there."

He pressed the brakes just as his car was about to swing into Old Mills Road. He didn't remember driving past the turn to Page's street. Something about that old road pulled him and, as he thought back, he realized he'd been drawn to the area—almost unwillingly—since his arrival in Mystic Ridge. Furthermore, something there connected him to Page. He was sure of it.

CHAPTER SEVEN

Fifteen minutes later, her doorbell rang. Quickly, she washed the taste of mint out of her mouth, dabbed some Dior perfume behind her ears and beside her nose and rushed to the door. She slipped the chain and the lock, and he turned the doorknob, stepped inside and she was in his arms. His grip, stronger than she'd known it to be, locked her to him and fear battled with excitement as his tongue slipped between her lips and dueled with her own. She tried to control him, to suck him into her and still the dancing torch, but he wouldn't give quarter, stroking and promising what he had in store for them. Her heart hammered out an erratic rhythm and shivers betrayed her body as he loved her with the sweet and wild torture of his tongue. Giddy with the aphrodisiac in front of her and all around her, she grasped his hips and rocked against him.

He moved her from him at once and spoke, tremors lacing his words. "I want to make love with you; I need it as I need air. But I want us to go away for a weekend, somewhere where we'll be on equal terms, and I want us to talk. Not about what we think and feel, but about who we are, what makes us happy and what hurts us. And when we leave there, I want us both to know what we need and expect from each other. I've been let down, and I know what pain is. I want to avoid both. Are you with me in this?"

She shuffled through the pages of her mind to try to figure out what he was talking about. Wasn't she in his arms and wasn't he taking her to her bed? Oh Lord, if she couldn't…if…

With a smile that told her he knew he'd practically hypnotized her, she asked, "When?"

"Does weekend after next suit you? You'll have handed in your report on the senior citizens. What do you say?"

She couldn't imagine anything more exciting than a weekend idyll with him, but she said, "I'll let you know in a couple of days."

His cool and solemn stare unnerved her for it was not in his character, at least as she knew him. "All right. I expect you'll call me and let me know."

"Oh, Nelson! Honey, I don't doubt what I feel for you, but when I take that step, the rest will be out of my hands."

"Do you trust me?"

Warm coils of comfort flowed from him, and she gazed into his eyes until tension danced between them like an unharnessed electric current, wild and dangerous.

"You don't have to ask that," she whispered, "because you know I'd trust you with my life."

He bent to her, claimed her mouth and unleashed the force of his passion until she was drunk on him as on a gallon of spirits.

When she could get her breath, she whispered, "Leave, if you're going."

He hugged her and, like a woodland sprite, slipped out of the door and left her there. Alone.

She'd have to work like the devil to finish that story, but she'd do it if she had to stay up nights for the next two weeks. Becoming lovers was not the only kind of intimate knowledge, and he was right in insisting that they experience every level of intimacy before committing to each other. He wanted her, but he didn't let his libido rule him. She liked that. With a light and happy heart, she went to bed.

Several mornings later, as she walked into her office, James stopped her. "Finding anything interesting at the senior center? I'd like to have an article for next week's issue."

She treated him to a withering look. "You serious?"

He had the grace to appear embarrassed. "Well...Uh...Yeah. I figured you could find something by now. You know, like how they spend the day."

"I'll do my best, boss."

"Now, Page, don't take it personal. I needed some information about the seniors, and—"

"I know. I know. It's never personal." She looked him in the eye. "Now, would you please let me work."

He held up both hands, palms out. "All right. All right. I just didn't want us to have any hard feelings over this." He couldn't match the hard stare she threw his way. Instead, he lowered his gaze and walked out.

Page sucked her teeth and looked at Phyllis. "A man breaks an egg and thinks he's done a great thing when he cleans it up. It never occurs to him that there's no longer an egg."

Phyllis bowed her head as though embarrassed.

"Sorry," Page said. "I forget sometimes that you two are sweet on each other and I open my big mouth. Oooops! I wasn't supposed to know that, was I?"

"It's all right. When I saw how you were with Nelson Pettiford, both of you so proud of each other and all, I was sorry I told James we had to keep it quiet. Now, he doesn't even take me out."

Page supposed her shock was obvious from her widened eyes. "You can't be serious. Girl, I wouldn't put up with that. Pick the most public place you can think of and tell him you want to go there with him. If he refuses, tell him you'll go with somebody else. He's single. Put his feet to the fire."

Phyllis stared at her. "Is that how you got Nelson to come here and get you?"

"No indeed. He asked if he should pick me up here or at home, and I said here and gave him this room number."

"Gee! He's not…I mean, people think he's…that there's something wrong with him, but there isn't, is there? And when you see him close up, he's real handsome. I never saw such gorgeous eyes on a man."

Page turned to face her. "He's been mistreated here. Because of his height, he's considered weird, and heaven knows what else. You know what the gossip is. But I paid no attention to that talk. He's a wonderful man."

Phyllis looked down at her hands. "I know I sound disloyal to James, but I don't blame you for not doing that story on Nelson. I could see he cares for you. That wouldn't be right."

"And I care just as deeply for him," Page said. "I don't want anybody to think I don't." She uncovered her computer, signaling the end of the conversation. Over the next two hours, she outlined her story of the plight of the seniors. Then she took her notebook and headed for the center to check some facts. At the corner, she bought a copy of *The Maryland Journal* and put it in her briefcase to read when she got home.

"See this?" Mrs. Cook asked her when she entered the Center. "I cashed my social security check right next door on my way in here this morning. That's nine hundred and seventeen dollars. I ain't spent a single dime, and now I got eight hundred and seventeen dollars."

Page consoled the woman as best she could, recorded the names of the workers who were in the center at lunch time. After she turned in her report, she'd pass that information to the Sheriff. She did the work she'd gone there to do and went home.

She changed to her favorite at-home costume—a floor-length T-shirt—got a glass of ginger ale, kicked off her shoes and remembered to call her mother. Her calendar showed that Millie was in Alexandria, Virginia, preparing for a town hall meeting. She phoned Millie's cell number.

"Darling, I'm so glad you called. You won't believe how distraught I am. Of all the nerve! If I ever get my hands on that person who calls him or herself Slim Wisdom, you'll have to bail me out of jail."

Page took a deep breath and prepared for the worst. Her mother did everything possible to garner publicity, any publicity, and tried to die if she got bad notices. "What's it about? I haven't had a chance to read the paper."

"Well, don't. It's disgusting, and just as I'm about to start my campaign for reelection. All I did was publicize the plight of hairdressers in Washington, and just look at this. It's so unfair."

She had planned to tell Millie about her story on the senior center, but as usual, Millie didn't have time to listen to any voice but her own. They spoke a few minutes longer.

"Well, I'm on in a few minutes, so I have to catch my breath. Are you doing all right in that little old town? For the life of me, I don't know why you'd prefer that to the Capitol where everything important goes on." She paused for a few moments, and Page knew the next words would come from her mother and not the public person Millie had created. "Be careful, child. You're a very tender person, and mother worries about you."

"I will, Mama."

The orchestrated Millie re-emerged at once. "My goodness, darling, I've only got two minutes. They gave me a dressing room two city blocks from the podium. I've got to run. Bye."

Page blew out the breath she'd been holding. Millie hadn't even bothered to find out why she'd called. One's own mother shouldn't be a source of stress, she told herself, as she opened her briefcase to get the paper. She stared at Slim Wisdom's political cartoon strip, Quigley, and steamed in fury. Why did every news jock consider her mother fair game? The phone rang, and she directed her ire to the caller.

"Hello!"

"Wow! Who watered the gas in your engine?"

"Nelson? Oh. Hello. I was just looking at Quigley. Do you ever read that stuff? Why's he always picking on women? That tomcat is the reason why I can't stand any kind of feline."

She wondered at the lengthy silence. At last he said, "Yeah. I see it all the time. What strip are you talking about? There's nothing in today's strip that's anti-female. At least, it didn't seem that way to me."

She threw up her hands. "What did I expect? Men in Congress do that sort of thing all the time, but if a woman does it, she's scandalized Capitol Hill."

To his credit, she thought, he refused to be drawn into an argument about it. "Page, I called to ask what you decided about our weekend?"

She thought for a minute. Oh, yes. Their weekend together. "Of course, I'll go. Why did you think I wouldn't?"

The silence was deafening. "I should have asked you that when we were together. If you're sure—"

She caught herself, because she knew she'd sounded flippant. But doggonit, her mind had been surfing elsewhere. "I'm sure, and I'm looking forward to it. Just let me in on the kind of weather I should expect."

"Warm weather and casual wear, but bring a couple of very dressy things."

"All right. How many days? I don't think I should ask for more than three or four."

"Four, if your boss will let you off, and bring your passport."

"He'll let me off, but you're kidding. Good Lord, honey, you're risking the white slavery law. You're not only taking me across state lines for the purpose of…uh…you know, but you're taking me out of the country."

"You got it, babe. If I'm gonna get thrown in the slammer, I intend to earn the right."

She fell back on the bed and crossed her knees. "I see you like to earn what you get. Works for me. I like to do the same, so if you're going to be so sweet, I'll have to cook you a gourmet dinner."

"Are you telling me you can cook?"

"You bet I can; otherwise I'd have starved. My mother can burn water and frequently did that. How about Friday night at seven?"

"I'll be there. Can I get my kiss?"

She blew him a kiss through the wire. "Good night, love."

"Till tomorrow, sweetheart."

Nelson hung up and stared at the receiver. Why would Page get so riled about that strip? Nobody could accuse him of denigrating women. And he didn't comment on them half as often as on men. Besides, he'd been gentle with the criticism. How would she have reacted if he'd ridiculed that woman the way he did Senator Thurman two days earlier? He flexed his shoulders in a slight shrug, called his travel agent and confirmed their reservations. He intended to make it work; it had to work. She was everything to him.

He walked into Page's house well aware that he hadn't previously been any farther into it than the foyer. She held his hand as he looked around her living room, hoping to broaden his knowledge of her through her tastes in furnishings. An enormous bowl of yellow and burnt orange chrysanthemums graced the large glass-top coffee table. A brown sofa, oversized beige and burnt orange chairs upholstered in velvet rested among Oriental carpets of complementary colors, and two enormous desert cacti dominated the room. He pointed to a painting of a group of jazz musicians.

"Who did that?"

"Doris Price. My mother has several of her things. The one below it is a reproduction."

"I like them. What gallery is she in?"

She told him and added, "It's amazing. We really do have similar tastes in art, except for drawings, and you promised to teach me what to look for in those."

He cleared his throat. *Best to get off that topic, especially in view of her reaction to Quigley.* "It'll be my pleasure." He sniffed the odor that wafted his way. "I smell something that's making me hungry."

"Like a drink?"

"Scotch on the rocks. A light one, please." She got a glass of wine and joined him. "Welcome to my home, Nelson."

He lifted his glass. "Here's to what nature had in mind when she made woman. Thanks for inviting me."

She seemed embarrassed and proved it when she said, "I...uh...better check the kitchen before I pull one of my mother's tricks and burn the dinner."

He watched her lithe body with its rounded, mobile hips glide seductively away from him and downed his drink. Spending an evening with her in her apartment wasn't such a good idea.

An hour later, with six courses of the best food he'd had in ages snug in his belly, he gazed around her dining room while she made coffee. White pillar candles of varying heights sat on the sideboard in a silver tray, the mirror above them giving their flickering lights added glow. And for the table she'd lighted more pillar candles and placed there a bowl of pink, white and purple dahlias. Feminine. Seductive. Like that lavender caftan that swished around her hips when she walked and outlined her high, generous breasts.

"You're quite a cook," he told her, walking with her to the living room where she'd placed a tray containing coffee and mints. "I take it you cook as a hobby."

"If you want the truth, I hate daily cooking. It's boring. I get a bang out of preparing interesting meals for guests, especially guests who, like you, enjoy eating."

"The meal was wonderful. Tell me about some of your other talents."

"I don't have any. I sing with a choral group, and…oh yes, I'm a fair quilt maker. I enjoy that."

"How do you find time to make quilts?"

"I haven't recently. Want to see the one I'm working on?"

She got up, hesitant he thought. "It's…it's in here." He followed her to her bedroom and realized why she's seemed reluctant to lead him there. The flames of more pillar candles glowed on the dresser, a delicate perfume teased his nostrils and his eyes beheld what was possibly the most feminine setting he'd ever witnessed. White walls, white furniture and deep pile white wool floor covering relieved only by the pink silk cover on her bed. The epitome of femininity.

She opened a closet door and took out the unfinished quilt. "I have a lot more to do on this."

He saw it and he heard her, but neither her words nor her handiwork registered. Her voice, sweet and soft, promised him heaven, and he stared at her as he willed himself not to get out of line, to remember the stakes. But he was full of her. Though she was halfway across the room from him, he smelled her, tasted her. As she folded the quilt, she glanced up at him with a smile on her lips, and desire slammed into him with the force of a sledgehammer. He whirled around and went back to the living room.

Inhale, count ten; exhale, count ten; inhale—

"What happened? Didn't you like my quilt? I mean, do you think quilting is old fashioned or...or something?"

"It's...it's fantastic," he said, gulping coffee. "I wouldn't have associated you with quilting. It must require a lot of concentration."

She walked right up to him, leaned over and placed a hand on his shoulder. "What's the matter? Anybody would think I aimed a gun at you. Why'd you—"

"Back off, baby. Will you? The quilt's beautiful. The dinner was wonderful. I love your home. You're lovely, Page. I've got to get the hell out of here."

"But—"

He stood and headed for the foyer where she'd hung his coat. "Listen to me, Page, and don't be hurt. Every vein, artery, muscle and sinew in my body is on fire for you, and the longer I stay in here, the worse it gets. What would surely follow isn't what I'd want for you or for myself. I'll call you when I get home." He opened the door, but she stopped him.

"Don't I get a kiss goodnight?"

He stared at her. "You're kidding. That would be the same as sticking a lighted match to a stick of dynamite. I'll call you."

Outside he leaned against his car and gave thanks. He'd been a hair's breadth from putting her in that bed and losing himself in her. And what a disaster it would have been, because he wouldn't have had an ounce of control. Never before had desire sneaked up on him, infusing him with such a powerful urge. Tremors raced through him when he recalled how close he'd come to destroying what he planned for them.

At home, he took a cold shower, put on a pair of pajama bottoms and a robe, went in his den and telephoned Page. He didn't dare phone her from his bedroom.

"I'm sorry I had to leave abruptly, but it was best. The evening was…well, it was magical."

"Are you sure there's nothing wrong between us?"

He hadn't expected such a question, and for a few minutes, he pondered what he might say that would make her understand. "I'm surprised I got out of there without making a dunce of myself. Honey, you pack a wallop and me…" he grinned as he said it. "Me, I'm just a man."

As he'd hoped, her laughter floated to him through the wires. "You're full of beans. If that's really the reason why you cut out of here, I'm going to start wearing denim."

"And what do you think that will hide? I'm talking about that whole scene you spun out there. If you're all right, I'll say good night. I don't dare ask for a kiss."

She blew one to him. "Good night, love."

" 'Nite, sweetheart."

He hung up and wiped the perspiration from his forehead. Thank God, she wasn't angry or pouting. Knowing that he wouldn't sleep immediately, he went to his den, tried some sketches, didn't like them and called it a night. The next morning, he stood beside his kitchen window sipping coffee and mentally planning his day. He'd been so wrapped up in Page, so comfortable in their relationship, that he'd almost forgotten how much he disliked going to the post office, to local stores and other public places where people gathered. Whenever he did, someone dampened his spirits with an incautious word or act, and he hated being treated as a curio.

On his way to the post office, he stopped at the library to return a book, but as he headed for the librarian's desk, two young women who seemed to have been shelving books pointed to him and giggled. He broke stride and walked toward them, but they scampered away. And a good thing, too, because he didn't know what he would have said to them. He thought he'd become inured to the cruelty, but could a man ever harden himself to ridicule? He turned and continued to the front desk.

The librarian beamed at him as he approached, a smile blanketing her face, and he turned around expecting to see someone in line behind him.

"Mr. Pettiford, I've been hoping you'd come in. We'd love to have you read for us and do a signing at the book store next door. Your books are very popular. We have a new readers' club that would be delighted to sponsor the event. If you don't want to read, you could talk about writing. We'd just love to have you."

Standing in that same spot, that woman had seen him at least twice a week for nearly two years and, until now, she'd managed never to look him straight in the face. And from her beet-red face and neck, he supposed his facial expression showed his astonishment and his indictment of her. He'd had the impression that the woman had never heard of Nelson Pettiford, author.

"Thank you," he managed with as much graciousness as he could muster. "I'll check my calendar and call you."

If her smiles weren't enough to floor him, she extended her hand. "This is wonderful. We'll look forward to the event."

Outside the library, he sat in his car wondering at the first impersonal gesture toward him as a man of worth that he'd experienced in Mystic Ridge. According to Whitfield, the mailman, everybody in town knew everything about everybody else, though that admittedly didn't include himself. He'd been seen holding hands with Page Sutherland, and it was as if some inexplicable transformation had happened to the townspeople of Mystic. Things had been decidedly different since the night he'd found her on the road. It was if she was the source of change. He shook off the strange notion and went home.

Seated at his desk, he shuffled through applications to his foundation. Two dozen young people had responded to the notice Page inserted in *The Mystic Ridge Observer.* He telephoned six applicants for additional information, but couldn't decide which had the most urgent need. He decided to work on his cartoon strip and then visit some of them.

An hour later, he looked over his effort, a piece in which Quigley expressed his opinion of members of congress.

"I'm more moral than you," Brother Tom said to Odessa-Cat. "I have family values."

"You sound like one of those TV know-it-alls, Brother Tom," Quigley said. "You're so boring. Always repeating yourself."

Odessa-Cat scratched her ear and turned to Quigley for sympathy. "How can he say that, the lazy tomcat, when he's the reason I've been fixed so I can't have any more fun?"

"Not true. Boys will be boys. I believe in family, the flag and God," Brother Tom replied. "If you liberal cats didn't prowl around in this alley all night, you'd still be intact."

"Oh, Quigley," Odessa-Cat moaned, "he's so cruel. Don't you remember all the…er…great times we had before—"

Brother Tom stuck his tail up, ready to prance off. "Please don't remind me of my wicked days, Odessa-Cat. I've been reborn. If only you liberals would see the light and stop worrying about these other broken-down cats. Let them stop having kittens, get a job and go to work. Then, maybe Providence will take care of them."

"Oh dear me, you must be running for president of Cat Alley," Odessa-Cat said. "I don't think I want to be reborn."

Nelson drew the cartoon in final form and put it in a mailer. After reviewing the six applications once more, he decided to make his first visit to the Mystic Ridge Group Home. The manager of the group home stared in astonishment when she learned that he was the foundation's benefactor, and he imagined how busy her tongue would be when he left there.

"I'd like to meet Ann. Of all the letters I received, hers, which you enclosed with your own, touched me most deeply. She wrote only four lines, but her misery jumped out to me." He smiled to put the woman at ease. "May I depend on your keeping my role in this confidential?" If not…" He let her imagine the consequence.

"Of course, Mr. Pettiford. You're a generous man, and we in Mystic Ridge don't deserve your kindness."

He lifted his left shoulder in a dismissive shrug. "I hope I can save Ann the humiliation she hinted at in her note. I could hardly believe a six-year-old could express pain so graphically."

"I'll get her. Please have a seat."

His heart nearly burst with pain, as the little brown-skinned girl with sad eyes who entered the reception room clung to the manager's hand.

"Hello, Ann. My name is Nelson. I read your note, and I can help you."

"With this?" She pointed to the patch of thick black hair that covered her brown cheek. "The children here laugh at me, and they won't play with me."

He took her hand and leaned toward her. "People laugh and make fun of me too, Ann, because I'm so tall. It hurts when they do that, so I know how you feel."

She gazed at him "You're tall? How tall?"

Did he risk standing? He decided to chance it, got up and raised to his full height.

The little girl stared up at him, obviously in awe. "Gee whiz," she said. "Gee."

He sat down. "Well, I can't do anything about how tall I am, but I can get a doctor to remove this growth from your face, and that side will be just as pretty as the other one."

"You can do that?" Her eyes widened. Lovely eyes, and she would be a beautiful child when that growth was removed.

"I can do that if you want me to."

She jumped up and down, slapping her hands together, and ran over to the manager. "Can he, Miss Dodd? He said he'll fix my face. Please, Miss Dodd."

Miss Dodd fixed stern eyes on him. "It's burden enough to be left here for whoever'll take you, but to be laboring under something like this…" She took a deep breath. "You're a godsend. How soon can you arrange it?"

"I'll call the surgeon today. Let's hope she has that pretty face by the end of the year."

He looked into the little girl's smiling face and laughing eyes, transformed from the sad child of minutes earlier. He hadn't felt so good in—he didn't know when.

"I'll be with you through every step of this, Ann. In a day or two, you'll know when the doctor can see you."

She reached to him with outstretched arms, and he leaned forward to receive her hug. A desperate hug that communicated her hope and her fear that nothing would change. The first hug he'd ever received from a child, and he had to control the urge to hold her close.

"Two weeks," the surgeon told him the next morning. "Why's it so urgent?"

"For a child, an hour is like a year. I've raised her hopes, and I don't want her to feel that I've let her down. Is there a chance that she'll develop keloids?" he added in a moment of apprehension.

"I'm not known for botched jobs, so don't worry about it."

Nelson thanked him and phoned Miss Dodd with the news. Feeling good about the world and everything in it, he checked over the tickets and reservations for himself and Page the coming weekend. He promised himself nothing would go wrong; he wouldn't permit it.

He walked out on his porch, looked up at the sky and let the wall take his weight at the sight of clouds that literally smiled at him. He went inside, but the vision lingered in his mind's eye and he went back to the porch. And still they smiled at him. The trees bent his way as if paying homage to him, and birds chirped and sang. Page, they seemed to say. Yes. He'd swear that every bird sang, "Page, Page." The townspeople may not have warmed up to him, but at every turn, Mystic Ridge welcomed him. Its sky, birds, trees and its Old Mills Road reached out to him.

CHAPTER EIGHT

Page zipped up her bags, placed them in the foyer and threw her raincoat across them. Standing before a floor-length mirror, she checked her avocado-green linen suit, inspected her three-inch-heeled shoes and took a last glance around her apartment. She'd watered the cacti, closed all the windows…Lord, she hated waiting, but he wasn't late. Her nerves had gotten so far out of control that she'd dressed early to give herself something to do.

The doorbell chimed, and with her heart pounding like a runaway train, she rushed to open the door.

Nelson stared down at her, and then a grin crawled over his face until it lit his eyes, and she knew everything would be all right. Lord, she loved his eyes. His lips brushed over hers fleetingly, but possessively, as if making a claim.

His smile turned to a grimace. "This all you're bringing?"

She glanced at the two twenty-two-inch bags and wrinkled her nose. "Well, you said I should bring two real dressy things. To me, that means evening wear, which takes up space."

"No problem. Ready to go?"

She nodded, and he set the bags outside the door, locked it and looked steadily at her. "Any second thoughts? If so, now's the time to tell me."

"None whatever. You haven't told me where we're going."

With his grin in place, stars danced in his eyes. "That's right. I haven't. You'll know when we get there."

"You're splurging," she said as they waited in the first-class lounge at Baltimore International Airport.

"Why shouldn't I give you the best I can afford? You'd do that for me." When she didn't respond, he urged her. "Wouldn't you?"

The man had a way of getting next to her when she least expected it. She winked at him, audaciously, in an effort to cover her flusteration. "I want the best for you, and I wouldn't offer you less than what was within my means." She patted the arm of the butter-soft leather chair. So they were traveling first class. She should have known he'd do that.

From the plane, they took a chauffeured stretched-out Town Car, and after a lunch of sandwiches and a glass of wine, she laid her head on Nelson's shoulder and went to sleep.

"Wake up, honey."

"We're there?"

"Well, partly."

She stepped out of the limousine and into swel-tering heat, removed the linen jacket and looked around to get her bearings. Her gaze fell on the mammoth cruise ship that loomed before them, and shifted to the eager expression on Nelson's face and his concern that his choice pleased her.

She reached up and hugged him. "Did I tell you you're wonderful?

"Are you sure it's all right?" he asked.

She couldn't figure out why he was anxious; her delight must surely shine on her face. "I've never been on a cruise or even on a big boat. This is…just wonderful."

He watched her as she twirled around in her stateroom. "You like it?"

Hope shone in his magnificent eyes, and she stopped dancing around and walked over to him. "It's beautiful, and I know the furnishings and accessories are not an accident. You had them decorate it similar to my bedroom." She waved her hand around to encompass the entire room with its white rattan furniture, white shag rug and pink spread and draperies. "I love it. Uh…where did the porter put your things?"

He looked down at his feet. "Next door."

"Well, I hope there's a connecting door between us."

His steady gaze with its age-old man to woman message nearly unglued her. "There is."

She'd worry about her sudden attack of brazenness later. "Okay. Scat. I want to put on something comfortable and then see what this boat looks like. Twenty minutes?"

"No kiss?"

She kissed the side of his mouth. "Out, bright spot."

"Right. I'll be on deck."

She looked out of the window at the deck, the small craft nearby, the ocean and the sea gulls. "Nelson, this is a dream world. It's…it's a fairy tale."

"I'm happy you're pleased. After half an hour of safety training we can explore this thing. We sail at five."

Three hours later, the Princess eased away from shore, bellowing her intentions as she pulled out. Page leaned against the railing in front of their state rooms with Nelson's strong right arm for her anchor. She looked up at him, then back at the receding shore.

"You're taking me on a cruise to give us a chance to know each other better. Where on earth will you take me on our honeymoon?"

She looked at him just in time to see his bottom lip drop and his eyes widen. But his shock apparently lasted only for a second. The fingers of his left hand tipped her chin upward as though to make certain that she not only heard his words but saw him say them.

"Marrying you is something I am neither willing to joke about nor to discuss lightly. My sense of humor does not cover that topic."

"Sorry." That sounded lame even to her, and maybe that was because his words sent a flush of delight throughout her body.

He moved away from the railing. "It's getting chilly. Shall we go in the lounge? What's your pleasure?" he asked, after they'd read the list of activities scheduled for the night.

"To sit here and talk with you." A smile played around his cheek bones, and she could see that her answer pleased him.

He ordered drinks. "I chose the second seating for dinner since I've noticed that you don't eat early."

"Fine." She reached over, took his left hand and examined it. Long tapered fingers with beautifully manicured nails and the smooth skin of a man who didn't use his hands for rough work.

"I like your hands," she said, unaware that she'd rimmed her lips with the tip of her tongue. "And I like their touch. Strong, but gentle."

At his silence, she glanced up to see eyes filled with passion and heat. Yes, and longing. Words she would have said hung in her throat as their gazes clung and she couldn't make herself look away.

"I like everything about you, Page. Everything. You take my breath away."

"Nelson, I—"

He waved his free hand. "Don't. I know it isn't the same with you, but if you'll let me, I aim to teach you."

She stared at him, bemused. How could a man be so blind? Or wasn't he able to accept that a woman he cared for could feel as deeply for him? *While he's teaching me, I'll bring him up to date on a few things.*

She stroked the back of his hand. "If it's not the same with me, why did I come on this trip with you, not even knowing or caring where you were taking me? You're a clever man. Figure that out."

His watch told him it was dinner time, but as they huddled close, holding hands in a quiet dream-like mood, he hated to interrupt the tender moment.

"Looks like it's time for dinner. Ready?" He took her hand and followed a crowd to the dining room.

They were seated at a table for eight with two couples and two single women. "How tall are you?" one of the men asked Nelson as soon as they'd introduced themselves.

Before he could react, he heard Page's voice slice through the air in a dagger-sharp reprimand. "Nelson's height will not be the subject of discussion at this table."

Stunned speechless, as their table mates also appeared to be, he stared at her with what he considered a silent caution. But she didn't back down.

"That's right. We'll enjoy our dinner if we don't get personal."

"Look, Nelson, I apologize. No offense meant," the man said, extending his hand.

"And none taken," Nelson replied, joining the man in a high-five.

He felt protective toward Page, had from the beginning, but it hadn't occurred to him that she might feel that way about him. He needed to sort that one out.

The waiters told jokes, sang, line danced and entertained the guests throughout the meal. His spirits high, he fed Page spoonfuls of caviar in between sips of champagne.

"You two must be newlyweds," one of the women ventured.

"Not yet," Page said. "On this trip, I'm just teaching him how to pronounce my first name. He insists on saying it with a French accent."

"But I thought you said your name is Page," the woman said with a note of uncertainty.

"It is," Page assured her. "Think what a problem we'd have if my name was Mary or April."

"All right. I get the message," the woman said, a sheepish grin on her face. "Nothing personal."

This was a side of Page to which he hadn't been exposed, this desire for privacy and the guts to insist upon it. He wondered at the reason for it. If he'd had any doubts that the cruise would give them a chance to know and understand each other, she had just dispelled them.

"Want to try the slots?" he asked Page as they left the dinning room, though he almost prayed she'd say no. He hated gambling, but they were supposed to be learning each other, so…

Her eyes widened and she stared up at him. "You mean the slot machines? Not me."

"Just checking. I don't gamble, but I wouldn't stand in your way if you wanted to."

"I don't gamble either, so…" She stopped walking. "Nelson, this is getting eerie. We have so much in common that it's beginning to scare me. And I'm starting to wonder why I chose *The Mystic Ridge Observer* when I also had job offers from *The Boston Globe, The New Orleans Tribune* and *The Baltimore Afro-American*. It's as if I was lured to Mystic Ridge."

He shrugged. "Maybe there's a reason why the place is called Mystic Ridge." He looked steadily at her, his mind racing. "I was watching TV one night, saw a short travel movie on Mystic Ridge, and I was ready to start packing. The place lured me the way a flame draws a moth. It didn't occur to me not to go there. Talking about weird! Let's sit over here in the lounge. It's cool on deck, and I'm not sure I want to join that frenzy going on upstairs."

They sipped the espresso coffee that he ordered and held hands as all kinds of people filed past them, but his mind was on Page's behavior at dinner.

"Why did you dress that man down when he asked about my height? Does my height bother you?"

Her stare was that of a person who'd been shot and couldn't believe it. "You didn't ask me that question. I don't wish that anything about you was different."

"Then why did you pounce on him so fast?"

"I'm sensitive to your feelings, and I'm tired of people who hurt others without thinking or caring."

"You didn't consider that I'd put him in his place?"

"If two men at that table had squared off, we wouldn't have had a pleasant meal. Right?"

"True." He rubbed his chin for a minute, deep in thought. "Are both your parents living? Tell me how you grew up."

She waited so long to answer that he wondered if she heard him.

At last, she said, "My mother's living, but not my father. I barely remember him, but I grew up in comfortable circumstances because my mother's a doctor. She's also something of a gadabout, attracts people the way sugar attracts ants. Since I'm an only child, I was always caught up in it, pulled from place to place—medical conferences, sorority meetings, speaking classes, trade shows. You name it. Loving though she is, life with her is one long stress scene. But what a woman she is!"

"She left you alone most of the time?"

"I wished she had. She dragged me everywhere she went; from the time I was nine, all I wanted was peace, a little calm and some privacy."

"But you love her."

"Of course, I do, and she loves me, but we aren't cut from the same cloth."

"I see." And indeed he did. "Where'd you grow up?"

"We lived in and around Alexandria. I moved to Mystic Ridge from Washington, D. C."

He settled back on the sofa with her left hand tucked snugly in his right one. "It's strange how different our lives have been and yet how similar in some important respects. My parents lived until I was grown, saw Logan and me through college and successful in what we'd chosen to do.

"They were older when we were born; we lost them a little over four years ago. Now, there's just Logan and me." His voice softened and suddenly seemed far away. "As you've no doubt guessed, they were both tall. Dad excelled at track and field, and he made a living as a lawyer just as Logan does. Mom taught music in the Baltimore public schools.

"Both you and I moved to Mystic Ridge seeking relief from notoriety, looking for peace and a private life," he went on. "After *Walking Tall,* my second book, came out, I was besieged wherever I went, and it wasn't all friendly. Taunts, jibes. That wasn't new to me, but that adults could be so…I'd as soon not go there."

She sat up abruptly. "So Rusty Orleans in your third book is actually you?"

He eased her back and into his arms. "Good Lord, no." She expelled a long breath in obvious relief. "He's a side of me, but the basic character is pure fiction."

"Boy, am I glad to know that. Now I understand why you established that foundation to help children whose handicaps subject them to ridicule. Did you get any responses?"

"A bag full. I've already chosen a six-year-old girl who has a growth on over a quarter of her face. When it's off, she'll be beautiful. I can't get her out of my mind's eye. Something about her—maybe it was the sadness when I first looked at her and the way she smiled at me when she left me—I don't know, but she haunts me."

"Will you let me meet her?"

He hugged her closer for she'd just said what he wanted to hear. "Sure, I will. Maybe we'd better turn in. Can I get you something first?"

She shook her head. "Nope. I'm feeling pretty good, Mr. Pettiford."

At her door, he asked her, "What time do you want to get up tomorrow morning?"

She looked him in the eye, letting him know with her cool regard that tonight wasn't their night. He didn't mind that because he knew the day's events had brought them closer. Much closer. And they still had a way to go.

"I want to see the sunrise."

"With or without coffee?" he asked, reminding her that he was right next door.

"Gosh, I hadn't thought of that."

He smiled to let her know that it was all right. "Knock, if you decide you want some, and if you don't feel like knocking, just open the door and come on in."

"You don't think I could forget that, do you? You'd better come inside and kiss me."

He looked down at the soft beige twin globes beneath the rim of the pink sheath that shielded the rest of her treasure from his eyes, brought his gaze up slowly to her glistening mouth and let his eyes feast on her luscious lips. He told himself not to look into her eyes and sink into the quicksand of desire. But he ignored caution, looked into those long-lashed grayish-brown pools of blatant need, and then her lips parted. He groaned, wrapped her to him and took the nectar from her mouth.

When she undulated against him, whatever she'd intended for the evening already forgotten, he broke the kiss. "Honey, do you want me to leave or stay?"

"Huh?" She hid her face in his shoulder. "I forgot where I was," she shuddered

That didn't surprise him. Gazing down at the bundle of feminine sweetness in his arms, he knew that she could bring him to his knees. "Go to bed, sweetheart. We have to get up at five to catch the sunrise. I'll phone you."

She kissed him under his chin. "See you in the morning."

CHAPTER NINE

Page fought the noise droning in her ear for as long as she could, sat up, looked around and recognized the noise as the telephone's ring.

"Yes?"

"Morning, sweetheart. I ordered breakfast, and the waiter will serve it on the deck beside our doors, so slip on something. Fifteen minutes?"

"Okay."

Fifteen minutes later, dressed in a yellow T-shirt and white cotton pants, she stepped out on deck where he sat in a deck chair with his hands locked behind his head and his feet stretched out before him.

"You're a cruel man; it's barely light."

"Come sit down. Here comes our breakfast table. Still think I woke you up too early?" he asked as the first ray of red streaked across the horizon.

"This is unbelievable," she said, as pigments of red, gray, orange and blue flashed over nature's palette. "Look. Oh, Nelson, just look at that," she said as the red globe slipped up from the Atlantic Ocean, a woman easing away from her lover's bed. "I wouldn't have missed it for anything."

She thought her heart would burst with joy, and she wanted him to feel the same way. "Are you…happy?" she asked him.

He reached over and squeezed her hand. "More than I've ever been or thought I could be."

"You're not an Aquarian, are you?"

A grin claimed his face. "Unless somebody changed the astrological charts, I am. February sixteenth."

"Then this isn't so strange after all. I'm a Libra, and I love Aquarians."

His laugh warmed her like steam from sidewalk grates on a freezing day. Suddenly, he sobered. "So you love Aquarians. What about this one?"

She got up, dusted crumbs from her pants and looked past him. "Why do you think I'd make an exception of you? Thanks for the breakfast. I'll be back out here after I shower and dress."

"And I'll be waiting for you."

"I never thought you could find so many things to do on a ship," she told him later that afternoon as they lounged alone on the ship's lee. "Imagine swimming, fencing and line dancing in the space of a few hours. I needed that movie in order to sit down and get some rest."

"If you're tired—"

She turned on her side and faced him. "I'm not so tired I want to leave you."

"What's your idea of the best way to spend Sunday?" he asked.

So he's still not satisfied that he knows and understands me. "Stick my arm out the front door, get the Sunday papers, crawl back in bed with a mug of hot coffee and read till I fall asleep again. Of course, I have to make the coffee first."

"And then what?"

"In Washington, I'd go to a museum, or write letters, watch the political pundits on TV, go to dinner or something special with a friend. In Mystic Ridge, I do the paper and coffee thing, take a walk, write letters, watch TV, do my laundry. How do you spend Sunday?"

"When I have my choice, I get up early, read the papers and eat breakfast. Then I go to church. I come back and call Logan or he calls me, and after that, I may work, garden, go for a drive, go over to Frederick and check out the antique shops, eat dinner and back home."

"You grew up in Baltimore?"

He nodded. "On the corner from Druid Hill Park. As a child, I spent a lot of time in that park."

She reached for his hand. "Alone?"

He sat up. "Yeah. Want some frozen yogurt?"

He didn't have to tell her that those had been painful days of rejection by children his age such that, even now, it hurt to speak of them. "I'd love some," she said and wished with all her heart that she could take all his pain away.

They walked back to their state rooms holding hands and eating double cones of frozen vanilla yogurt.

"The captain's giving a party tonight. Want to go?"

"You bet I do. I brought these evening dresses, and I'm going to wear them even if I have to put them on for breakfast."

He raised an eyebrow. "And you'd do that, too. Get some rest, why don't you? I'll knock at seven thirty."

She waited for the kiss that would send her spinning, but he let a grin play around his lips. "Oh, no you don't. I'm drunk enough just looking at you." He kissed her cheek. "Later."

He looked around the tables at the captain's dinner for first-class passengers and counted his blessings. On this night, he was just like other men of his status, enjoying the company of a beautiful woman whom he loved, who cared for him and wanted everyone to know it. On this night, he was not wishing for what he deemed impossible nor trying to pretend that he didn't need it.

"Dance with me?" he asked her, as the orchestra whipped into an old Duke Ellington ballad about what it meant to be blue.

She stepped easily into his embrace, with the confidence of a woman who knew what she wanted and took it. Her supple body moved against him, her steps matching his as if they had danced together all their lives. He stepped back from her so that he could focus on the music, on anything except the way she moved against him, but she closed those few inches and let him feel her breasts, her hips and her lover's promise. He held her away from him and gazed into her eyes trying to clarify her message, to know for certain what she intended to communicate. For a second, she let him see her need, then her long lashes closed that window and she moved back to him. But not before he saw the tips of her hardened breasts beneath the silk that barely covered them. He stopped dancing.

"Do you…want to…Can we leave here?"

"I want to go wherever you want to take me."

"And if I want to take you to my room?"

She took his hand turned toward the exit, and with his heart rioting in his chest, he followed her.

She didn't stop at his door, but led him to her own. His gaze seared her with the fiery storm of desire in his eyes, and as her trembling fingers slid the plastic card through the lock, she said a few words of prayer. *Lord, please let him know and feel that I love him.* She flipped on the light and waited for him to close the door behind him, but as though being sure of his ground, he left that task to her. She closed and locked it.

"Want some champagne?" she asked him, pointing to the bottle of Moët et Chandon that rested in a bucket of ice on her dresser.

He shook his head. "I'm not leaving unless you ask me to." Wasn't it typical of him to eschew small talk and get down to cases. However brazen she acted sometime, she wasn't really aggressive with men and she hoped he'd figure that out. How did you deal with a man who'd known little else but loneliness? She made herself say, "I haven't planned to ask you to leave. Don't...don't let me just stand here. Hold me."

He stepped closer. "There's no turning back for me after this. You understand? I'm deeply in love with you and when we make love, I'll only sink deeper. Do you love me?"

"Oh, yes. I love you. I've never loved anybody else."

She sensed the air bursting out of him, air that she knew had sought expulsion probably for decades. A smile enveloped his face, and his eyes shone as though sheltering millions of stars. His arms opened and she flew into them and gloried in his masculine strength as he crushed her to his body. His lips found hers, and she opened to him as he poured into her the fever that raged in him. She parted her lips and feasted on his tongue, welcoming him into her body. His fingers gripped her hips and when she undulated against him, he raised her to his level, pushed aside the shoulder strap of her gown and sucked her hard nipple into his mouth. The hot molten lava of desire shot through her, and she moaned her need aloud not caring that he knew how she longed to have him inside of her. She held his head to her breast as he teased and suckled, making her will his own, until in disregard for all but the feel of his mouth on her, she lowered her other shoulder strap and pushed her evening gown down to her waist.

As he moved from one breast to the other, she threw her head back and moaned, "Put me to bed; I can't stand this."

A gasp escaped her when he slid her down, and her belly skimmed over his powerful erection. His deft fingers unzipped her dress and tossed it onto the chaise lounge. Then he lifted her and carried her to her bed. He pulled back the cover, lay her in bed and his eyes feasted on the treasure that awaited him, hidden only by her slim bikini panties. Staring down into her eyes, he threw off his clothes and knelt beside the bed. His lips seared her belly and her inner thighs as he peeled the little G-string from her body. Frissons of heat singed her nerves as she felt his gaze on her naked body.

He joined her in bed, leaned over her and streamed kisses over her face, neck, ears and shoulders. "You're so sweet, so…Oh, God, I love you!"

Then he had her nipple in his mouth tugging and suckling until her hips swayed of their own volition as her need for him threatened to explode

"Honey, please, I…"

"I've waited all my life for this; let me enjoy loving you. I need to love you this way." His lips trailed down to her belly where he sipped, kissed and nipped until she thought her whole body had burst into flames. But he continued his onslaught, kissing his way as he went until he reached the ultimate, hooked her legs over his shoulders and loved her until she screamed for more. He took a minute to protect her.

"All right, baby," he said, rising above her. "Tell me if I hurt you."

She shifted her body upward to meet him and took him in her hands as she stared into his face and brought him to her lover's gate. He touched her and her body became a raging storm. The clutching began when, at last, he sank into her and she couldn't hold back the tears. Tears of joy that at last he was hers. She smiled to let him know her joy and, gazing into her face, he began the powerful strokes that sent jolts of electricity whistling through her veins to settle in her love nest as he rocked her. Almost immediately, the squeezing and pumping began, and he drove relentlessly while she thrashed beneath him, wanton and beyond control.

"Love me," he whispered. "I need you to love me."

"I do. I do. I love you so much."

His lips touched her in a possessive kiss as he increased his pace and power until she buckled under him in a shattering eruption. Then he wrapped her in his arms and cried aloud as he gave her the essence of himself.

His body shook with the power of his release, and he had to control what he felt for her lest he hold her too tight. With his elbows and forearms supporting his weight, he let himself relax, opened his eyes and gazed down at her in wonder, awed that he held in his arms the perfect complement to himself.

"How do you feel?" he asked, his voice little more than a whisper.

Her smile was all the answer he needed, but her words soothed him. "Wonderful. I didn't know I could feel like this. Is…Is everything all right with you?"

"As never before in my life. I'm…to think that I might never have met you."

Her fingers stroked the side of his face, caressed his chin and then brushed over the tight curls on his head, loving him, cherishing him, and he'd have sworn that she could hear his heart thundering its mad rhythm. He stifled a groan. No matter how their song played out, he would love her forever.

Her grin told him to expect irreverence and she made good the promise. "If my car hadn't acted up, we wouldn't be here right now."

"At Gayne's Garage, where you took it, I was told there wasn't one thing wrong with your car. That entire event smacks of the supernatural. I tell you, it's creepy."

"Say what you please, my car is entitled to your gratitude."

Encouraging her frivolity, he said, "Convince me."

"Well, people get a physical examination every year, and—"

"Okay, I'll take it for another tune-up. That ought to square things."

She feigned surprise. "I hadn't even thought of that; I was thinking more of an oil change, but if you want to go that far..." She let the thought dangle when he spread kisses over her face and neck, brushed the tips of his fingers over her breasts and then sucked an aureola into his mouth. When she wrapped her legs around him, he shifted his hips and took her with him to the stars.

Nelson walked into his house that Monday evening, dropped his bags in his bedroom and looked around him. Nobody could tell him that he wasn't a brand new man starting a brand new life. He telephoned Logan.

"I thought you'd decided not to come back."

"I was only gone four days."

"How's Page? Did you take her with you?"

He didn't lie to his brother, the person who'd always been there for him. "We were together, and she...she's just fine."

"Great. Way to go, brother. Stay on top of it."

"If I don't, you can bet it won't be my fault."

"I thought as much. Why don't you come over next weekend?"

"I may camp out at your place a few nights. I told you about Ann, the girl my foundation is helping, didn't I? Well her surgery is scheduled for next weekend, and I think I ought to see her through it. I'll let you know more later this week."

He hung up and called the surgeon. "Is the operation still on?" he asked after they greeted each other.

"Yes, I was at the group home yesterday morning as promised, and I examined her. I don't expect any problems. Bring her in Thursday afternoon. I'll operate at seven thirty Friday morning. If all goes well, she should be out of there Tuesday or Wednesday, but I want her where I can watch her to see that she heals properly. If you don't know of a place, I can recommend one."

"Go ahead and make the necessary arrangements. I'll have her at the hospital Thursday."

After telephoning Miss Dodd and getting her cooperation, he sketched a few cartoon strips. In spite of what he planned to draw, his pen insisted on depicting Quigley strutting down Old Mills Road toward the lake. Finally, he let the big tom have his way.

"I'm getting too old for this night prowling," Quigley said. "I need a cozy little nook with a cozy little cat."

Nelson stared down at what he'd drawn and gasped when he saw that the little cat had Page's face. He tore it up, phoned a Chinese take-out for his supper and thought over the weekend while he waited for the delivery. After their first night together, he and Page hadn't wanted to be away from each other and had spent the remaining two nights in each other's arms. And that last evening at the gala, she had been so breathtakingly beautiful that he'd seen the envy of other men. For once, he had the prize.

He'd had the company of any number of beautiful women, but he had been with them as ships passing through the night. And they, dangling themselves before him as precious jewels, had proved to be mere plastic at the core. He'd known no pleasure in being with them. He hadn't loved any of them nor had they loved him. Liaisons of convenience, all of them. But with Page, his soul had soared. He put on his coat and went down to the gate to get his supper from the delivery man. After eating, he phoned Page, talked with her for a few minutes and went to bed.

After lunch the next day, he went to visit Ann, to reassure her and tell her what to expect. She walked into the reception room, looked around and when she saw him, her face bloomed into a smile and she raced to him with open arms. He stooped down and lifted her into his arms. To his amazement, she kissed his cheek. Deeply moved, he kissed the ugly birth mark on her face and hugged her. When he sat down, she sat as close to him as she could while he outlined her treatment program.

"You're going to be there?" she asked him, her voice filled with hope.

"I'll be there, and I'll take care of you. You must be patient while your face heals and do exactly what Dr. Mack tells you to do."

"I will. Dr. Mack brought me some lollipops. He has a little girl, too."

"I'll come for you day after tomorrow."

The fierceness of her hug communicated to him more aptly than any words what his gesture meant to her. After apprising Miss Dodd of the arrangement and getting her agreement, he left, whistling as he strode with quickened steps to his car oblivious to the cold and biting wind. First Page and now this wonderful little girl lit up his life. He'd do his best for her.

CHAPTER TEN

Sitting at her desk across the small room from Phyllis, Page dialed the third number she had for her mother but got no answer. Fearing a tragedy, she called Millie's secretary.

"Dr. Shipley is in Mexico City, Ms. Sutherland, which is why you couldn't reach her by cell phone. She'll be back tomorrow."

Relieved, Page hung up. What business did a congresswoman from Virginia, United States of America, have in Mexico City, Mexico? She knew her mother loved to travel, but justifying some of her trips required a magician's skill. She hadn't spoken with her mother since she'd gotten back from that unbelievable idyll with Nelson. Thinking of him and their days and nights together, she hugged herself, remembered where she was and looked into the knowing eyes of Phyllis Watson.

"That had to be some weekend. You were a can of mush all day yesterday, and you're still pie-eyed. He must be some hot stuff."

Sobering at once, Page raised an eyebrow. "Since I didn't hear you say that, I don't have to tell you whose business you're meddling in, do I?"

"Sorry, girl. I didn't say a thing. But I've been trying to take a leaf out of your book. James took me to dinner at the Wild Duck right here in Mystic Ridge, and on a Sunday night, too. Can you beat that? I had it out with him, and he's been acting different."

"A man will give you what you let him know you deserve."

"I'm crazy about him, Page."

"If he floats your boat, go for it."

Phyllis stopped typing. "Do you love Nelson?"

"Would I love the most perfect, most precious human male the Lord ever made?"

Phyllis' lower lip dropped and her wide eyes stared as if seeing a supernatural being. "You get outta here, girl."

Page couldn't help laughing—at the astonished woman before her and because the whole world was new and wonderful. Her feet barely touched the floor on her way to her boss' office.

"Here's your story on the seniors, James."

He glanced at what she'd placed on his desk and, displaying little interest in it, motioned for her to sit down. "Still don't intend to get me a story on Pettiford?"

She'd thought that issue closed and said as much. "You've already penalized me for that. Anyway, before you decide to get tough with me, read my story. I think you'll change your attitude toward both me and the seniors."

His eyebrows shot up. He picked up her story, looked at the heading and began to read. Half an hour later, he walked into her office. "All right. I'm taking you off features and putting you on news, and you get a couple hundred bucks more in your check every month. You done good."

"You going to leave me alone about a story on Nelson?"

His gaze drifted toward Phyllis then back to Page.

"I'm not a louse, kid. I know how you feel about him. I'll get it myself."

"Can I thank you for that?" she asked Phyllis after James went back to his office.

"Maybe. I don't know. I did ask him how he'd feel if I did an expose on him? That could have had an effect."

Page walked over to Phyllis and hugged her. "Thanks, friend. I couldn't have done it, not even if he'd fired me."

Nelson put Ann's small suitcase in the trunk beside his bags and prepared to drive to Baltimore. "You're welcome to come with us, Miss Dodd," he told the manager, who stood by anxiously as he buckled the little girl in the back seat.

"Can't I sit up there with you?" she asked him.

Fortunately Miss Dodd explained that state law required children under twelve to sit in the back seat, for he wasn't sure he could have denied her request.

He talked with her on the way and learned that she had rarely been in a car, that she loved music and reading was her favorite entertainment. How like himself as a child, he thought, living inside herself, shunning rejection. If only he could help all children who were burdened with being different. He checked her into the hospital and sat with her in her room until she slept because she'd begged him not to leave her.

He'd also chosen two other children, but he already knew that neither of them would touch him as Ann had. He stood by her bed at seven the next morning when attendants placed her on a gurney and anesthetized her and realized that he couldn't have been more anxious for her if she'd been his daughter. He got breakfast at the cafeteria, went to the gift shop and bought toys, a radio with a cassette player/recorder and several books of fairy tales. That done, he went to the waiting room, took out his sketch pad and made himself work.

Three hours later, Dr. Mack's voice came to him, a shadow emerging from the darkness as he sat staring at his empty sketch pad. "It's about as perfect a job as perfect can get. When the sedation wears off, she'll be in pain, but I've left a prescription to take care of that." Mack patted him on the shoulder. "Man, you're something special. That little girl is going to be a beauty."

Nelson said a word of thanks and used his cell phone to call Page.

"She's going to be just fine," he told her. "Waiting for the doctor to come out nearly drove me nuts. I'm going up to see her now."

She told him of James' reaction to her report on the senior center. "I'm senior staff reporter now. No more features. He's going to try and get an interview with you himself."

That wouldn't be unreasonable. "Perhaps in connection with my lecture at the Mystic Ridge Library, though I don't know when that will be. I'll call you tonight. Love you."

"I love you, too, hon. Bye."

For the next four days, he sat with Ann during her waking hours, sketching while she read the books he brought her, and it pleased him that she always wanted to discuss with him what she read. He discovered that she delighted in Mozart's chamber music and in boisterous pieces such as Tchaikovsky's Romeo and Juliet, and that she loved the music of Louis Armstrong and Pete Fountain. His taste as well. Nursery rhymes held no interest for her. He didn't know much about children, but it hadn't occurred to him that a child would dislike the simple tunes that were written for children.

He marveled that she didn't complain of pain, showed no restlessness or impatience and raised no objection when he told her she had to recuperate at Dr. Mack's sanatorium.

"I like Dr. Mack," she said. "He fixed my face."

If Page were with him to share his happiness about Ann's successful surgery, he'd be complete. He phoned her. "I miss you. I haven't seen you in a week. Can't you come over this weekend? You can stay with Logan and me, but if you'd rather stay in a—"

"I'd rather stay with you and Logan."

When he could stop laughing, he said, "I hadn't envisaged your staying at a hotel by yourself, sweetheart."

He imagined that she raised her eyebrows when she replied, "Neither did I, love. One week couldn't make me that crazy."

"Glad to hear it. I want you to meet Ann. With her calm acceptance of what is happening to her, her faith in those responsible for her care and her almost unbelievable equanimity, she is a revelation. I've learned much from her."

"I want to see her too; I can tell she's become very important to you."

"You think so?"

"I know it, and it's good. See you Friday night."

"Hey, woman! Where's my kiss?" She blew him one through the wire, and he told her he loved her.

"Me too, love."

"Wait a second. I'll have a car to pick you up at your office. Five o'clock?"

She hesitated. "Well, if you want to, but I don't mind driving."

"I mind. See you then."

Logan thought Ann would be jealous of Page, but the little girl embraced Page as one more person to love her just as she had opened her arms to Logan. The three of them stood by Saturday morning while the surgeon removed the thin gauze from Ann's face and handed the child a mirror.

She stared at herself and looked at Nelson. "Is this me, now?"

"It's you, and you're beautiful," Nelson told her.

"Not quite," Dr. Mack said. "That side will soon be exactly the same color as the other side."

"It's really me?" she asked Nelson again. As stunned as she, he sat on the side of her bed and hugged her. He wouldn't have imagined that she would be so pretty.

The surgeon gave Nelson instructions for Miss Dodd and discharged Ann. Nelson and Page gathered the toys, books, cassettes and other things Nelson had bought her, packed her things and left the sanatorium with Logan and an ecstatic Ann dancing between them.

The three adults had their first taste of Kentucky Fried Chicken, because that was what Ann wanted to eat.

"We'd better head home, Logan," Nelson said. "Thanks for the hospitality and moral support."

After belting Ann in the back seat, Nelson walked around to the front passenger door and looked down at Page. "The more I'm with you, the more I never want to be away from you. Give that some thought, will you?"

She took his hand and brushed the back of it against her cheek. "I have."

His heart kicked over like a trip-hammer nearly knocking him off balance. "Did you think I hadn't?" she asked.

He braced his palms on the roof of the car, trapping her between himself and the vehicle, and leaned down until his lips touched hers and he felt her body, warm, pliant and for him alone.

"It's broad daylight, and we're on the street," she said, pushing him away.

"Yeah. That and Ann are what stopped me."

"You coming to see me soon?" Ann asked them when they were leaving the group home.

"You're part of my life now, Ann," Nelson said. "You can always count of me."

She hugged the two of them. "Nobody will be mean to me any more," she said and, as she waved them good bye, her smile warmed him like rays of sunlight.

He took Page's hand and walked with her to his car. As he got in, he said, "Somebody left her on the steps of the group home when she was a couple of days old. If only that man or woman could see her now! You know, I changed her life, but she changed mine more."

"How so?"

"She brought home to me the extent of my enormous blessings. A comfortable home, parents and a brother who loved me. And now…Imagine, being able to give someone a new life. It's…I'm humbled."

"She loves you."

"I know. And it's mutual."

It was time he told Page that he was Slim Wisdom. She'd been annoyed at one of his strips and maybe he'd do some more that she wouldn't like, but she deserved to know. And then, he'd…He'd cross that bridge when he got to it.

"Where've you been, darling? Mother's out of her mind. Two whole weeks, and I've—"

"Mama, back up, will you? You knew I was going on a trip, though I admit I didn't say to where. When I got back home, I called every one of your phone numbers, but you didn't answer any of them. Then I called your secretary and learned that you were investigating something or somebody in Mexico."

"Now, dear, don't be so exacting. I was on a fact-finding trip. Unfortunately, it's something we congress people have to do in order to legislate."

Yeah. Sure, she thought but she didn't say. "What did you decide about the next election?"

"What's there to decide, darling? The people are pleased with my work, and I'm going to make a run for it. I hope I may count on your vote."

Page laughed. She couldn't hold it back. Her mother's public persona was in full swing and nothing short of victory in November would slow it down. Maybe then, she'd have her mother back. But Millie could switch personas as easily as the wind switched directions.

"You didn't tell me where you were going, dear? Did you have a nice young man with you?"

She hadn't been expecting that one. Gathering grit for whatever comeback she got, she said, "I was with someone special, Mama, and I didn't tell you where I was going, because he made the trip a surprise."

"I uh…I see. Where did he take you?"

"On a cruise to the Bahamas and neighboring islands. First class all the way. If you come visit me, I'll introduce you to him."

Millie's long silences didn't fool her. She knew that in matters of romance, her mother remained old fashioned and disapproved of casual affairs. "You love him?"

"Yes, ma'am. I love him."

"Well, well. He must be Superman. I'd begun to think I wouldn't live to see it. You bring him here to see me. You hear?"

"I will, if I can catch up with you," she said, getting some of her own. "Bye for now."

"Wait a minute. I'm going to Ghana Wednesday afternoon, but I'll be back Monday morning."

"You're going on vacation, or what?"

"Now, dear, you know the price of cocoa has been rising for months, and I have a big candy factory in my district, so I have to see what's what over there?"

"But Mama, what can you do about it?"

"I can protect my constituents."

In West Africa? Page stared at the telephone for seconds after she hung up. "I guess that's that."

Thursday morning, Phyllis dropped a copy of *The Maryland Journal* on Page's desk. "Girl, just look at that. I cracked up. Slim is da bomb!"

Page grabbed the paper and stared at the cartoon strip and the caricature of her mother on Millie-Cat's face, as the feline took off in the air with nothing to propel her but inline skates on each paw and a long scarf trailing behind her.

Odessa-Cat complained to Quigley, "That little alley strumpet isn't satisfied with the Toms here in Cat Alley. She's gotta go prowling clear out of the country. I could wring her neck."

Quigley looked at his friend and former lover, closed his eyes and licked his lips. "Your eyes have gone green, Odessa-Cat, but you're wasting good hate. Millie-Cat hasn't been in heat in twenty years. All she'll get for this trip is a reality check."

Soothed, Odessa-Cat stretched and purred. "If you ever run for president of Cat Alley, Quigley, I'm voting for you."

Page pitched the newspaper into the refuse basket and swore aloud. If she ever got her hands on that…that miserable person, she'd…

"Didn't you think it was funny, Page? Slim's got his finger square on the political pulse of this country. I think he's…Page, what's the matter? Why're you looking at me like that? What did I say?"

"Every time you open your mouth, I see your big toe."

"What? Well, kiss my grits. I never in my life! Page, honey, you sure you're all right?"

"No, I'm not. See you tomorrow," she said, closed her computer, got her briefcase and went home.

She couldn't blame the reporters and comedians for taking shots at her mother; it was their job. Besides, politicians were fair game. If only her mother wouldn't do such outrageous things in order to stay in the limelight. She wouldn't be surprised if Millie went bungee jumping in a corset and old fashioned bloomers to call attention to gender inequality and, of course, to herself. Oh, Lord, how she wished her mother would just be a normal mother. A doctor, yes. A congresswoman, yes. President of the United States, if that's what she wanted. But a normal mother.

She had no taste for lunch, so she forced down an apple, took out her laptop computer and tried to work on her story. She answered the phone thinking she'd hear her boss' voice.

"Hi, sweetheart. What're you doing home this time of day? You okay?"

"Hi. I'm working on a piece for this week's edition."

"Whoa. I'm not sure I've ever had this frosty a greeting from you. What's bothering you?"

"Oh, hon. I'm glad you called. I really am. But I'm so mad right now, I couldn't be civil to Dick Clark and Ed McMahon if they showed up here with one of their big money checks."

"What happened?"

"Why are these vultures always picking on…on…on women. I get so sick of that damned Quigley, I could spit."

"What? You let yourself get this upset about a cartoon that doesn't have anything to do with you? That's the silliest thing I ever heard."

"Silly? Did you call me silly? Is that what you said?"

"Now, look. You're just looking for a fight."

"You insult me, and when I object, you say I'm looking for a fight. How dare you make light of me?"

"Page, honey, for heaven's sake, don't be childish!"

"Childish?" Bang. She slammed the phone into its cradle, and for the next fifteen minutes, her tears soaked her shirt. Christmas was only days away and with her mother likely to take off on another junket, she'd probably have to spend it alone. She made a cup of tea and curled up in a big over-stuffed chair contemplating what she'd done. Never had she hung up on anyone. Anger and remorse battled for priority, and she shuddered at the thought that he might not forgive her for it. She clutched her chest at the frightening tumble of her heart. Then the doorbell rang, and she wrestled with the impulse to ignore it and with an urge to be in his arms, for she didn't doubt that he'd come to have it out with her.

He rang again. "Open up, Page. I'm not leaving here until you do."

She slipped the chain and opened it. "You knew I'd be here, didn't you?" he said. "What got into you?"

She stared up at him, looking for…she didn't know what. A sign of the sweetness he always gave her, maybe, but she didn't deserve it. "Come on in. I'm…I'm sorry I hung up on you, but I'm still mad at you for calling me silly and childish."

With both hands on her waist and his gaze locked in hers, he said, "I didn't come here to rehash that scene."

"Why'd you come?"

"Because I love you and you love me, and this is too precious to allow an argument about something like that to get between us."

"But I'm still—"

He interrupted her. "You're not mad at me any more than I'm angry with you. We were both wrong." He searched her face. "You've been crying? Page, baby, don't you have any faith in us? In me?"

His hands stroked her back and folded her to him in a gentle caress. "What we feel for each other can't be destroyed so easily."

"I…it was an awful feeling. Suddenly, I didn't have you any longer."

"Shhh, sweetheart. In a world of cyclones, this wasn't even a breeze."

She wanted him to stop talking, to wrap her to him and let her feel him, taste him. She raised her arms to his shoulders and lifted her parted lips for his tongue, and he gazed down at her until his body jerked and his hot male magnetism sucked her into his aura, mesmerizing her and firing her libido until she wanted to scream at him: Do something to me. Touch me. Kiss me. Hold me. Get inside of me.

"I told you there was no turning back, and there isn't." Then he plunged into her mouth, dipping, seeking, tasting and anointing.

She imprisoned him with her loving tongue, dueling frantically with his own until, at last, he fastened her hips to him and bulged against her. Weakened with the desire that plowed through her and settled in her loins, she slumped against him. Then, he lifted her into his arms and took her to bed where, together, they made the earth stand still.

Later, as he held her, he thought about his life and gave thanks for it, even the empty years, for without them, he might not have appreciated how precious she was.

CHAPTER ELEVEN

Nelson waited in the reception room of the group home while Miss Dodd signed the permission for him to take Ann for a drive, their fourth excursion together. He drove down Old Mills Road, as he'd done previously, parked and walked with her through the thicket to the edge of Lake Linganore. Squirrels darted in their path and when Ann knelt to play with one, he stood still and watched her while she stroked his fur. Nelson couldn't believe what his eyes saw. Maybe he was bewitched. Or was it simply more of the strange power of Mystic Ridge?

They sat on a bench facing the lake, because she loved the view, and the squirrels played at her feet while she squealed with delight. She wanted to know about his childhood and he gave her an edited version of it. The hour passed quickly, and he hated to take her back so soon; those minutes with the little girl brought him a new kind of happiness. Her face had healed and, true to the surgeon's promise, she'd become a beautiful child. He stopped at a roadside restaurant and bought them each a double cone of caramel ice cream.

"Right on time, Mr. Pettiford," Miss Dodd said when they returned. "Punctuality counts for a lot here." Ann hugged him goodbye and asked him when she'd see him again.

"Over the holidays for sure," he said, not realizing that the child might have her own agenda for Christmas.

"I'm going to ask Santa Claus to bring you something," she told him and hugged him goodbye.

He planned to celebrate Christmas with his brother as usual, because he assumed Page would want to spend it, or at least part of it, with her mother.

"I assume you'll spend tomorrow with your mother, but how about going with me this afternoon to see Ann. It's Christmas Eve, and I want to take her gifts."

"Wonderful. I have something for her too."

"She won't come out," Ms. Dodd told them. "She says she doesn't want to see you."

He supposed his face showed his disbelief. "That's impossible. I haven't seen or spoken with her since I left her here in this room three days ago. What happened?"

"Well, she asked if she could spend Christmas Day with you at your house, and I told her the rules forbade it. Your taking her to the hospital for surgery and caring for her later in the sanatorium was special, but otherwise the children have to stay here."

He sent his fingers ruthlessly through his hair. "Granted. But why is she mad with me?"

"She thinks you didn't want her to visit you. I tried to talk to her and tell her it was a group home ordinance, but she wouldn't listen. She's pouted and been…well, just plain bad ever since."

"I see. Would you please take these to her? We'll wait."

Miss Dodd returned with the gifts a few minutes later. "She said she didn't want them, and she wouldn't let me leave them with her. I just can't figure out what's come over her. She's always been such a sweet, obedient child."

"Maybe if we mail them to her and don't put our names on them, she'll accept them. It's Christmas, and I don't care who she thinks gave them to her as long as she gets them," Page said.

He walked from one end of the reception room to the other and back, his right hand gripping the back of his neck. "But how?" Why hadn't he thought of it? He snapped his finger. "The post office is still open. We can get Solomon to bring them in the morning." He turned to Miss Dodd. "She doesn't have to know who sent the gifts. Santa Claus could bring them. I just want her to have a wonderful Christmas."

"You're a good man, Mr. Pettiford. She sure won't learn it from me."

"She'll get them, but I don't feel good about it," he told Page as they left the post office.

"She loves you, Nelson, and she's hurt, but she'll get over that as soon as she misses you."

"I hope you're right. I…poor thing. She's had such a difficult life. If only…No point in iffin'. We'll drop my place first and then yours to get our bags, and head for Baltimore. Logan's roasting a goose."

Logan greeted them in his white apron and chef's hat. "Why don't I just put your bag in Nelson's room?" he asked Page. "Then you two won't have to be tipping around in the dark knocking things over and waking me up."

Nelson glared at Logan in a chilly reprimand. "I know you pride yourself in saying what you think, so I advise you to do something about your mind. You embarrassed Page."

"He did?" Page asked.

Nelson glanced toward her and his eyes widened. Whatever he'd expected, it wasn't the wide grin and wicked glint he saw in her eyes. He threw up his hands. "Oh, you two! Do whatever you want."

After a feast of oyster stew, roast goose, wild rice, fluted cremini mushrooms, turnip greens, corn muffins and brandy-alexander pie, they strolled along Charles Street for a few blocks enjoying the lighted trees and myriad other seasonal decorations.

"Don't you have a girl?" Page asked Logan when they returned home. "I hate to think of you alone, especially at Christmas time."

"It's been almost two years," he said, "but the loss is still so fresh that I can't reach out just yet, but I'm making progress. Having you with us this Christmas takes away some of the loneliness for me, and I know I don't have to speak for my brother. Isn't it time you two made this permanent?"

It didn't surprise Nelson that she looked directly into his eyes then quickly away. When they got back, he'd tell her about Quigley, though he knew she'd spout fire, but he hoped she'd get over it quickly, because his work was his life.

"You'll be the first to know," Nelson said.

"I'm glad to hear it," Logan replied. He dimmed the lights of the ceiling-high Christmas tree, and put on a CD of carols. "Let's open our presents."

Logan received an elegant briefcase from his brother to replace the one Nelson claimed disgraced the name Pettiford. Page gave him an audio note taker with a ninety-minute tape capacity. Her gift to Nelson was a bound set of Mozart's music for wind instruments, a CD of Paul Robeson ballads and an album of Fats Waller's complete recordings. Logan's gift to Page was an album of photographs from Nelson's childhood, and he had a set of fishing gear for Nelson.

Page unwrapped the bottle of perfume Nelson handed her and stared at him. "How did you know this is what I wear?"

He pointed to his eyes. "I had occasion to observe."

"Ahem," Logan said, clearing his throat. "Leave something to my imagination, brother."

Nelson couldn't help laughing. "Oh, I did. Believe me, I did." He put his hand in the pocket of his jacket, pulled out a small parcel and handed it to Page.

"You said you'd been thinking about it," he said, as she stared in awe at the diamond solitaire. He knelt on one knee. "Will you wear it and will you marry me? You know how I love you and can't stand being without you."

Her face betrayed her bewilderment, and she shook her head as though afraid to believe her ears. "You're asking me to marry you?"

He nodded, unable to speak, for fear his heart would fly out of his chest.

Stars danced in her eyes and the smile on her face seemed to light up the room. "Oh, hon," she said, slipping to her knees in from of him, "Yes. Yes. Yes." She wrapped her arms around him, and he had to fight back the tears.

After a few minutes, she nibbled at her lower lip, and he knew he could expect an audacious word or act. She stood and looked down at him.

"Oh dear, I said yes, and you didn't make me a single promise. A girl's suppose to work this for all it's worth." She turned to Logan. "Isn't that right?"

Logan's face bore a look of pure joy. "There's still time; he hasn't put the ring on your finger."

She looked at Nelson with raised eyebrows, her expression prodding; she waited.

"I'll love you as long as I breathe. I'll take care of you and be a good father to our children." He thought for a minute. "Oh yes, and I'll take you to Tahiti on our honeymoon."

"Nobody's supposed to know that but…" Her bottom lip dropped. "You're kidding!" She held out her left hand. "Put it on before you decide you can't afford that trip."

He slipped the ring on her finger and sealed their commitment with his lips pressed to hers.

"I'm turning in. See you in the morning," Logan said. Nelson sat in the big chair and patted his knee. "You're so far away."

She came to him, gliding along in slow motion it seemed to him—though she was only a few steps away—and sat on his knee. He slipped his arms around her and held her tight to his body.

"If anybody had told me a year ago, that I'd be sitting here Christmas Eve night with my future wife in my arms, I wouldn't have believed one word of it." With a smile that made his heart sing, she raised her face for the loving he needed to give her.

After lunch, Christmas Day, he called Miss Dodd. "Did Ann get her gifts?" he asked after they greeted each other.

"Oh, yes indeed. Mr. Whitfield brought them around ten this morning, and she danced and laughed and hugged him. But Mr. Pettiford, I'm afraid she thinks the presents were from Mr. Whitfield."

"I don't mind that so long as she has them. I thought I'd stop by this afternoon."

"Uh, maybe not. After she saw the toys and played with them a little bit, she sank right back into that sad, distant way she acted before her plastic surgery. I don't know what to do."

"What about the social worker?"

Her snort surprised him. "Ann can't stand her, and I'm not enamored of the woman. Tell you what. I'll get the Board's approval and bring her to your place for a visit on my day off, if it's all right with you."

"Wonderful. Just let me know when."

The child's behavior worried him. If he could have celebrated Christmas with her for only a few minutes, he could have relished more his new status as a man about to be married to the woman he adored.

He met Mr. Whitfield at his gate the next morning, Tuesday, and asked him about Ann. "She's a beautiful child, so sweet, but I thought there was something sad about her."

"Yeah. Well, thanks for getting those presents to her on time."

"My pleasure. Here's your papers and your mail. Plenty of it today." Whitfield tipped his hat, adjusted his bag and continued his rounds.

Nelson went through *The Washington Post* first, then *The Maryland Journal.* He'd told himself that he'd leave women alone for a while, since Page got out of joint when he made fun of them, but he couldn't pass this up: Millie Shipley's antics were front page news again. In the name of Kings, what could she find in South Africa at Christmas time after just coming back from Ghana, when the cost of travel was at its peak, that she had to know in order to draft legislation or vote intelligently on a bill? He sketched Millie-Cat purring up to a proud male lion, she with the face of Millie Shipley and he the personification of Thabo Mbeki, South Africa's president.

"I guess Millie-Cat thinks she's too good for us toms here in Cat Alley, not that we're missing anything," Quigley said to Odessa-Cat.

"Not to worry, Quigley, my dear, the big lion's in for a surprise. All Millie-Cat wants is to get her picture taken with him so she can come back here and show it to us. The hussy is frigid," Odessa-Cat said, swished her tail and raised it to its full height. "The little strumpet will do anything to get noticed."

Quigley licked his paws and yawned. "And to think, I used to fantasize about the little wench." Nelson touched it up, drove to the post office and mailed it.

The next evening, speaking by phone, he and Page agreed to eat dinner together at his house. "I'll cook," he said. Little did he dream how much he would regret the idea.

"I hope you don't get shook up about this one," Phyllis said to Page that morning as she handed her *The Maryland Journal*. "This strip just blew my mind. Face, it Girl, Quigley is inspired genius."

She looked at it, closed her eyes and counted to ten. "I'm not going to react," she told herself, knowing that Phyllis watched her. *If Mama wants to make a fool of herself, it's no skin off my teeth.* Though boiling inside, she draped her face in serenity, pushed the paper back to Phyllis and went on with her work.

That evening, Page rang the bell at Nelson's gate at the same time as he appeared around the house racing to let her in. Her breath seemed to stall in her throat as he swung it open, gazed down at her and grinned before picking her up and swinging her around.

"Hi. You're early. I'm just getting the stuff together."

His lips brushed her lightly, but she didn't care, for she knew there was more to come. Much more. "My watch crawled along so slowly," she said, "that I figured something was wrong with it."

In the dusk of evening, their laughter mingled as they wrapped an arm around each other's waist and strolled to the house.

"Make yourself at home while I do this," he said as he whisked egg whites. "It is your home after all," he added.

She studied the paintings and drawings in the wide hall that had the appearance of a gallery. Jacob Lawrence, Doris Price, John Biggers, Elizabeth Catlett and Romare Bearden, the greats among contemporary African-American artists, were represented. Nelson was obviously a man with fine artistic taste and the means to indulge it. Through a doorway, she saw a bass fiddle leaning against the wall. Curious, she walked in to examine it and gasped aloud. There, on a large easel, was a drawing of Quigley in color. She stepped closer and saw on the draft board a Quigley cartoon in progress.

Her fingers trembled as she reached out to touch it but snatched back her hand as chills shook her and she nearly convulsed in pain. But then anger took over and she had to deal with her jagged breathing and the fury that churned in her. She charged back into the hallway and got her coat.

"Where're you going?"

"Home. This was all a mistake." She slammed out of the door, slipped the lock on the gate, got in her car and went home. How dare he make a fool of her mother!

Nelson turned off the stove, dumped the uncooked food into the garbage disposal, got a beer and went into his living room to sort things out. She hadn't thought enough of him to explain, and he wasn't going to crawl on his knees and beg. Loving a woman didn't mean you had to be her door mat. Out of habit, he flipped on the TV. Several reporters and cameramen at Ronald Reagan International Airport in Washington caught his attention. Then he saw her.

"What do you fellows want from me? I gave up Christmas with my only child, my Page, so I could make the trip while Congress was in recess. I tried to do what's right, and you…you snoops try to make me out a criminal, to turn my efforts to cement relations between our two countries into a calamity, a cause célèbre. I'll bet a quarter of the Congress went off on fact-finding missions this season, but you pick on me." She tossed her head and walked on. "Go do your dirt somewhere else."

He lunged forward. Why hadn't he noticed it before? Those eyes and that voice. Carbon copies. Millie Shipley was Page Sutherland's mother, and he was in trouble. He sank into the sofa. What a mess!

After a sleepless night, he got in his car and drove all morning trying to think, his one hope being she hadn't given him back his ring. Shortly after noon, he drove to Page's apartment.

"Please open the door, Page. I'm not leaving until you do." She cracked the door and he walked past her before she could ask him to come in.

"Why didn't you tell me she's your mother?"

"Why didn't you tell me you were Quigley…I mean Slim Wisdom. I hate that cartoon. Do you hear me? I detest it."

"Political cartoons are my livelihood. How would it look if I took stock of every off-the-wall thing in Washington, and ignored Dr. Shipley, when she's one of the most conspicuous actors on Capitol Hill? She's never once written me and complained."

"You're not even sorry you made a fool of her, are you?"

"I made a fool of her? If she didn't do all these crazy things…Look, I didn't come here to argue. One of us had to make the first move, and I'm making it. I'm sorry if you're hurt."

"You could at least promise not to do it again."

He stared at her. "You're asking the impossible. You want me to forfeit my impartiality, the thing that gives me authority as a political commentator. You can't ask that of me."

"You're saying no?"

"Yes, and I won't ever change."

She walked to the front door and opened it. "I'm sorry. You don't know how sorry I am."

He didn't pause, but walked out as quickly as he could. Pain shot through him, but he'd get over it. He walked into his house and heard the phone in his office ringing.

"Mr. Pettiford, this is Miss Dodd. Have you seen Ann?"

"Have I seen…You don't know where she is?"

"No. I took eight of the children to the library this morning, and I thought she was with us when we got on the bus to come back, but she was nowhere. I'm out of my mind. I've called the sheriff, and all he said was 'Don't worry, we'll find her.'"

It didn't take a genius to realize the child had run away. "I'll do what I can to find her. Here's my cell phone number. Please call me if you learn anything. Miss Dodd, that child is precious to me."

"I know that, Mr. Pettiford. I'll stay in touch."

He hung up and dialed Page's number. "Baby, I know you're upset with me, but I need you. Ann's missing." He explained what he knew.

"My Lord, she's run away."

"That's what I think. I'll be by your place in half an hour."

"I'll be ready."

Nearly ten hours, and she hadn't been found. His belly pinched and squeezed him, empty for want of lunch, dinner and water, but he couldn't think of food and drink. He looked over at Page as he retraced one more place they'd already searched. "Do you want me to get you something to eat?"

She shook her head. "I'm not hungry. Do you think she's been kidnapped?"

"No. She ran away. I'm sure of it. Oh, heck, I must be getting addled; I meant to turn into Boyers Mill Road. Out here on Old Mills Road is the last place I'd expect to…" He heard a staccato noise that appeared to come from the engine.

"Now what? I had this car tuned up a couple of days before Christmas." The engine sputtered once more, and the car came to a standstill.

"Just what we need."

They got out of the car, and he lifted the hood to examine the engine. "I'm sorry you have to spend New Year's Eve this way, but I…I don't know what I'd do if anything happened to that child. She got next to me the first time I saw her with those sad eyes and—"

"If we weren't looking for Ann, I'd say this is a great way to spend New Year's Eve," Page said. "Did you ever see such a moonlight? No wind. It's…well, if she's outside somewhere, at least she won't be in the dark, and she isn't cold." She looked around. "Hey, do you realize this is almost the exact spot where my car stalled the night we met?"

"You think…Look honey, someone's coming. An old man walking along with a German shepherd dog. Well, it was worth a try."

"Sir, we're trying to find a little girl. She's six years old and about this high." He bent over to show the man Ann's height.

The man gazed at them for a minute. "Over this way," he said and patted the dog on the head. "Come on, boy."

They followed their guide through the thicket and, suddenly, his heart did a drum roll. He'd taken Ann there on each of their outings. Why hadn't he thought of that; she loved to go there and look at the lake. They emerged from the brush to the shore of Lake Linganore and the dazzling sight of the lake, ethereal with the full moon aglow above it, and the shadow of the silvery cylinder dancing in its waters.

A gasp from Page brought him to her side. "What is it, love?"

"It's so touching, so otherworldly. Not a bit real. I…" Suddenly, she squinted at something beyond him, for her gaze had followed the old man. "Nelson! Good Lord! Look!"

He raced to where the child lay on a bed of leaves, dropped down on his knees and placed his ear to her chest.

"She only sleeping," the old man said. "She's perfectly all right."

Nelson looked first at Page, who knelt beside him, and then at the old man. Then he bowed his head. "Thank God." To the old man, he said as if in after thought, "And you. How can I thank you?"

The old man half smiled. "Don't worry. You thanked the right source."

He led them back through the thicket and, as they emerged, snow flakes so thick they could hardly see ahead of themselves fell all around them but not on the three adults, the child and the dog. Nelson opened the car and laid Ann in the back seat.

"Now if I could just get this thing started," he said to Page as he went to open the hood. "I'd gladly give you a lift, sir, but I can't get this buggy to start."

The old man shrugged and patted the big dog that stood close beside him. "Put the key back in the ignition and turn it."

Nelson's head snapped up. That was an order if he'd ever heard one, but he did it and the engine hummed. He got out of the car to thank the man and repeat his offer of a ride, but, there in the brightest moonlight he'd ever witnessed, he saw only empty space. He stepped to the road and looked both ways, but saw no one. Not even a shadow.

"Who...hooo." A hooting owl. He hadn't heard one in years. He walked back and forth along Old Mills Road checking the bushes, looking for any kind of movement. Nothing. No one. He rushed to the car and looked in the back seat, certain that it had all been an illusion. But Ann lay where he'd placed her. Rubbing the back of his neck, he looked to the sky. Then he shook his head and got in the car.

"Can you beat that?" he asked Page, as he drove toward Mystic Ridge. "Do you think we dreamed up that man?"

Page looked in the back seat to make certain that Ann was there and what they'd thought they experienced wasn't an apparition. "Honey, let's just be thankful that we have her and she's all right. She's still asleep." She turned to face the road. "Uh...do you believe in angels?"

"I didn't, but now I'm not so sure. What time is it?"

She looked at the iridescent hands on her watch. Five after twelve. "Happy New Year, darling."

"Happy New Year, sweetheart. I'll kiss you when we get home. Okay?"

"Okay," she said, and he let out a long breath. He handed Page his cell phone and gave her Miss Dodd's number.

"We found her, Miss Dodd, and we'll be there in a few minutes."

"Thank the Lord and hallelujah," the woman said.

Nelson drove on to Mystic Ridge, more slowly now, aware that the pain and fear he'd shared with Page as they searched the town and countryside for Ann had tightened their bonds and strengthened their love for each other. He glanced at the woman by his side and gave silent thanks.

He carried Ann in one arm, and with the other, tucked Page to his side as they entered the group home. Standing just inside the door, he made up his mind, walked over to the sofa in the reception room and sat down. Ann clung to him, her fingers gripping his arm and her eyes wide with panic.

"Can't I ever come to your house? I want to stay with you sometime."

He tucked her close to his side. "Sweetheart, if you'll agree, I'll see about making that permanent."

Wide awake now, she stared up at him. "You...you mean—"

"I'd like for you to be my little girl and live with me all the time."

"You mean adopt me and you'll be my daddy?"

He looked at Page, and her smile of agreement sealed his resolve. "That's exactly what I mean, and you'll even get a new mother."

He'd never seen such happiness as the glow of the little girl's face. "My name is going to be Ann Pettiford. Now, it's just Ann," she said, giving him a fierce hug.

Nelson took Ann's hand and walked over to the desk. "Do you have papers here for initiating adoption proceedings, Miss Dodd?"

She clasped her hands before her. "I sure do. Well, well. You don't know how happy this makes me. It's the right thing, and I'll vouch for you." She paused. "Oh dear. A little girl and you being single and all."

"That won't be for long," Page said, looking up at her husband-to-be with loving eyes. "We're getting married, Miss Dodd."

Miss Dodd beamed with delight and handed Nelson the adoption papers. "Bring them back soon as you can."

He took out his pen. "How about right now." He turned to Ann and winked.

"I'll get it started first thing tomorrow," Miss Dodd said. "I tell you, the Lord works in mysterious ways, His wonders to perform."

"Happy New Year, Miss Dodd," they chorused.

"Yes. A blessed New Year. And congratulations to you both." She put an arm around Ann's shoulder, and they waved good-bye.

Half an hour later, Nelson led Page into his den. "Have a seat. I'll be back in a second."

She looked around. Quigley was still there on the easel and a work in progress graced the drawing board. It was the strangest thing, but it suddenly occured to her that Quigley looked just like that cat on Old Mills Road the night she first arrived in Mystic Ridge. She was determined not to worry about the things she couldn't explain, and just accept the fact that things simply happen in Mystic.

Nelson walked in with a bottle of champagne, a bag of potato chips and a can of peanuts. "We have to settle this first. Then I'll gladly cook."

She tried to breathe, but she only panted. "What is there to say?"

"You're ashamed of your mother, and I realize that's the reason why you left Washington and came here, why you didn't tell me who she is and why you haven't taken me to meet her."

"I'm not ashamed of her."

"Then I take it you approve of her capers."

"I don't, and I...I want her to grow up."

"There you have it, honey. You have to learn to accept her just as I had to learn to accept my height, to see its advantages and stop worrying about wise-cracking characters. Your mother is a woman of singular achievements, a physician and a congress-woman, a person who makes the laws of your country. Honey, try to stop sitting in judgment on her. This is the twenty-first century and everything has changed, including women's roles. Can you accept her for who she is?"

"I don't have a choice. When she's in her private persona, she's a loving, caring mother, but when she's being her public self, she's outrageous."

He chuckled. "Personally, I like some of those wild things she does, though I have to needle her when she pushes the envelope too far."

"When we get married, are you still going to do those awful cartons about her?" she asked, pretending to pout.

He had to laugh. "Uh…yeah, and I'll bet she makes sure I get the information. We love each other, baby," he said, pouring champagne in two long stemmed glasses. "I want to spend my life loving you, but I won't be happy without my work. Can we set the date?"

She nodded her head vigorously. "I guess you're right about Mama. She loves the limelight. She said she wanted to meet you, and I'll take you to her this weekend." He locked arms with her, and they sipped the cold champagne.

"I love you, sweetheart."

"And I love you."

He put their glasses on the cocktail table and bent to her waiting lips, lips now starved for his sweetness. She gripped his shirt as his tongue found its home deep in her mouth and shivers raced through her. She placed his hand on her breast and he broke the kiss.

"You're not hungry?" he asked her.

"I'm hungry for you."

He picked her up, carried her to their bed and to that other world where only they had been.

THE CHOICE

BY MONICA JACKSON

Poor Evelyn Sweet never thought she'd have a love of her own, and that selfish family of hers wasn't helping matters any, that's for sure. Our final tale shows how the spirits of Mystic changed Evelyn, and those fast-talking sisters of hers, too. They still talk about what happened, but only whisper it in the privacy of their home. Evelyn thought she was going plum crazy, but there wasn't nothing crazy about Evelyn Sweet. It was just changes coming...

CHAPTER ONE

Evelyn Sweet dropped her shopping bags on the couch and followed them. She eased low-heeled pumps off her feet and tried to rub the soreness away. The shopping mall had been a madhouse with the usual rush of people doing last-minute Christmas shopping. She'd always done her Christmas shopping early to avoid dealing with the crowds. But there had been a flurry of hints from her daughter and younger sisters about stuff they'd wanted and had to have. She was scared to see what her credit card statements would look like. A twinge of anxiety struck her about her bills.

She'd got the week of Christmas off work for the first time in her fifteen years of tenure as a registered nurse at the hospital. Instead of looking forward to the holidays, she was starting to dread the endless cooking and preparations. These sorts of thoughts nagging on the tired edges of her mind were unwelcome. Anxieties and a sense of dissatisfaction. Nope, thoughts of gratitude for her blessings, giving, and generosity were the sorts of things she tried to fill her mind with. She had health and the love of her family and friends. What blessings could be greater than those?

Evelyn moistened her lips. Suddenly, they felt like they'd been touched. Something like tender kisses. A masculine, musky scent wafted around her own longing. Evelyn frowned and stood. What was wrong with her lately? It was almost five o'clock. She had to get dinner started.

Cars always surrounded Evelyn's neat, but nondescript, vinyl-sided white ranch around dinnertime in her working- and middle-class neighborhood. Dinner was a drop-in affair and well attended—her sisters and their kids would be there. Her sisters might bring their men of the moment. Friends from work might drop by, or folks from church.

Evelyn cooked and catered and cleaned up after them as well as she could. Folks seemed to think her cooking was pretty good because her table was always full of people and she loved it. Didn't she?

She put the bags in the closet and went into the kitchen. Her kitchen was the heart of her home and she loved it. It was straight from the fifties with big white old fashioned appliances and white enameled metal cabinets with red trim and a big kitchen table to match. Her one extravagance was the black granite counter tops she had installed. She spent a lot of time in this kitchen and it suited her.

Evelyn had decided to cook smothered pork chops for tonight's dinner. She got the extra-large family-size pack out and reached in the cabinet for the seasonings. Suddenly Evelyn cocked her head and listened intently.

She heard singing. Smooth and soulful, like gospel music. Did she leave a radio on somewhere?

"There you go cooking on the white folks' part of the hog again."

Evelyn spun, her heart freezing. "Who's there?" No answer.

She started to take a step forward and stopped, biting her lips nervously. There had to be an explanation. Of course there was. She cocked her head and listened. The homey and familiar hum of the refrigerator and the tick of the wall clock were the only sounds she heard. She was tired. That had to be it.

Evelyn bent over and put the big frying pan on the stove. Her eyes moistened. It was December 17. The anniversary of Sweet Mama's death was a week away. The grief had faded to a dull ache, but with her fatigue and the memory of her loss last Christmas…No wonder she heard her great aunt's voice, the woman who raised her and her sisters with a firm but loving hand.

The white folks' part of the hog. Sweet Mama liked the pork chops, the ham and the bacon, but she loved the parts of the pig reserved for the black folks way back when. Smoky ribs and crispy fried pigskin. Pig's feet and chitlins. *That's good eating, child,* she would say. *We took the scraps and turned them into gourmet cuisine. That's how we black folks do it.*

"Evelyn? You in the kitchen?"

"Yes, I'm back here, Deb."

Her youngest sister glided in, sniffing. "You scared me for a moment. I didn't smell any food."

"I just haven't got it in the pan yet. I know you all would riot if I didn't cook."

Deb was beautiful, trim and small with smooth skin that looked like honey and long black relaxed hair hanging over her shoulders and down her back. Deb favored her other two younger sisters and her mother's sister, Aunt Jean. Not for the first time did Evelyn wonder why she'd gotten such a different set of numbers in the gene lottery, with her stocky body, dark skin and short, kinky hair.

Her mother and grandmother had drowned together in a flash flood so long ago that Evelyn's memories of being clasped to a full, soft chest by strong arms were all that remained of them besides a few photos. If it weren't for her looking so much like Sweet Mama and the old photos of her mother, she would have thought there had been some mistake.

Fair or dark, plain or pretty, the family legacy is always the same, Sweet Mama would say. Evelyn had frowned because that usually was a prelude to Sweet Mama going on and on about the importance of choices and dirty-doggish men. But everyone in Mystic Ridge knew that Evelyn's choices had already been the wrong ones.

"Pork chops? What are you cooking with them?" Deb asked.

"I'm making smothered pork chops, rice and gravy, sweet peas, yellow pound cake. Speaking of peas, they're in the refrigerator. You can snap them for me and put them on to boil with a pinch of sugar and lots of butter."

Deb heaved a sigh and went to the refrigerator. "Sometimes I wonder why I show up early and don't have the sense to wait for the food to be on the table like everybody else."

Evelyn shrugged, and unaccustomed resentment touched her. She was forever cooking and tending to other folks. What would it be like to come home to a good meal for a change? She banished the thought.

"Let me tell you why I rushed over," Deb continued. "I had to tell you the news. You aren't going to believe it. David's back in town."

"David?" Evelyn put a questioning tone to the name, but she knew who he was. Her heart thudded as she remembered the handsome young man whom every single girl in the town wanted to call her own. They'd gone to school together, first through twelfth grade. Not only was he the best-looking, most athletic young man with the highest test scores and grades, he was also one of the nicest boys she'd ever met. David Douglas had been born under a lucky star.

"I know you remember David. That man was so fine, when he left, the echo of breaking hearts around this town about broke the sound barrier."

"He went into the Foreign Service after college, right? What makes him decide to finally bring his family back to Mystic Ridge after all these years?"

"This is the good part, sis. He was in a car accident in Germany, serious injuries, and his second wife booked on him."

"That's the good part?"

"The man is unattached, broken-hearted and has been injured. He comes back to his hometown to heal and nurse his wounds. What could be better? He's ripe for the picking. The man is mine, do you hear me?"

Evelyn shot a sharp glance at her sister and shook her head. "The poor man," she murmured under her breath. "You were a kid when he left. What do you know about David?"

"I remember David quite well. And I'm not a kid anymore."

Evelyn started to open her mouth to reply when her daughter Ashley bounded in, all long legs and coltish energy. "Hi, Mom."

Ashley glanced over at Deb. "What's going on, Aunt Deb?"

"We were talking about David," Deb replied.

"Who isn't? It's so romantic. Wounded hero returning home…"

"As far as I know Germany isn't a war zone anymore, and the Foreign Service hardly qualifies as military duty," Evelyn said dryly.

"Mom, you know what I mean."

Evelyn eyed her daughter, hardly believing that this tall beauty sprang from her loins. Ashley was home from the University of Maryland for Christmas break. She was staying in her own apartment and just dropping in occasionally. Evelyn barely got to see her. The apron strings were fraying. She'd be ready to graduate next year and she was already talking about heading off to the West Coast for grad school.

Ashley was both the best and worst thing she'd ever done her entire life. She'd been a child having a child when she gave birth to her at fourteen. She could scarcely believe what was happening to her and to her body. When she brought forth this little wailing creature, she'd stared at it in disbelief.

"You've set a course for your life, child. You gave away your youth and you're a woman now," Sweet Mama had said.

And that was the way it had been. From that moment on, she'd been a mother to her child and her three younger sisters. She'd never looked back.

Her heart ached at the thought of her baby grown up and gone. Time had gone by so quickly. She was only thirty-five and she felt like a much older woman who'd never had the fiery juices of young womanhood fill her.

An hour and a half later, dinner was on the table. Folks were talking all at once and enjoying their food thoroughly. Evelyn hurried between the kitchen and the table, as was her habit, refilling glasses and serving platters, bringing out dessert.

Janet said, "I asked David to dinner over here tomorrow."

"Why?" The word from Deb was a sharp rap.

"I thought it would be a nice gesture."

"A nice gesture towards what?" Deb bit into a roll. "Don't get any ideas, now. That man has my name on him."

"I think it is a very good idea to be welcoming toward David," Beverly interrupted. "The man has been through so much."

"And Deb here is itching to put him through more drama," Janet said.

"You got that right," Deb replied.

Evelyn went in the kitchen and closed the door behind her, shutting off the exchange. Her sisters kept a friendly rivalry going on between them over men. It had always been like that since they were teenagers, but they'd never seriously stepped on each other's toes. Beverly had been out of the loop with her marriage, then the bitter divorce such a short while later. Evelyn was happy to see her rejoin the banter. Apparently nobody ever considered that Evelyn could be interested in a man or that any man could be interested in her.

Although Deb's words had been joking, she'd obviously decided that David would be one of the very few men around Mystic Ridge worthy of her. Janet saw a catch too. Plenty of women would be after David Douglas—that was for sure. It should be interesting around Mystic Ridge with him back, and the Lord knew this town needed all the excitement it could get.

That night Evelyn woke suddenly to the whistling of the wind and cold so frigid her breath made white, ghostly puffs in the darkness of her bedroom.

She shivered and got out of the bed, drawing the blanket tightly around her. She slipped on her house shoes and made her way to the thermostat.

The heater kicked on immediately and she moved back to her bedroom to burrow under the warmth of the covers.

She stopped. Was that a voice she'd heard? "Sweet Mama?" Her voice quavered and hung in the cold dark air.

Evelyn stifled the urge to turn on every light in the house and get back into bed. Remnants of a dream? A whisper from the grave? The hairs stood up on the back of Evelyn's neck. She sat up in the bed and reached out for the lamp. The yellow light from the lamp warmed her and she drew her knees up to her chest and wrapped her arms around them. The voice of Sweet Mama should be nothing to fear. If only she could hear her voice again, one more time. If only.

She picked up her watch by the bed stand. 12:03 and the date was December 18. Exactly one week before Sweet Mama died the year before on Christmas Eve. It had ruined Christmas for everybody, but Sweet Mama never put much stock in the holiday anyway although she claimed to love the time of the year. Fool commercialization, she'd murmur. Santa Claus and trinkets and spending too much money. Old gods own that time, and don't you forget it.

The longest, darkest night of the year.

Evelyn's head snapped up. "Sweet Mama?" she whispered. There was a hint of pleading in her voice. She needed her now. Sweet Mama was the only one who'd cared for her in the way Evelyn gave and gave to others. Sweet Mama would cook the things she liked, rub her back and tell her to keep on putting one foot in front of the other when it seemed as if the world was against her. She missed her so much, and the year's passing had hardly dented the rock of her grief.

Evelyn cocked her head and listened hard. Was there the thrum of drumbeats, women's voices raised in joyous song, or was it the hum of the heater? Was she losing her mind?

She buried her face in her hands. Evelyn had thought this Christmas would be easier—a time of healing and renewal after the sad Christmas of last year. She'd wanted to make this Christmas special. But she was exhausted and broke and getting broker. Everything was falling on her, as usual.

Her home was the hub of the family. She poured the money, time and energy to keep the traditions and family spirit alive, and her home was where they all gathered. Four sisters, their men all gone or lost, and their children. They all lived in Mystic Ridge, tied there by reasons of circumstance and habit. A family of women was what they'd always been, and family was all Evelyn had. All that was supposed to matter. Why the hole in her heart?

"Sweet Mama?" She needed her so much.

She turned off the light and lay back and closed her eyes. She felt sleep wash over her.

"Rest, child. You rest now. There's changes a comin' soon."

CHAPTER TWO

Evelyn awoke with a start, feeling chilled to the bone. She gathered the bedcovers close to her and glanced over at the clock. It was six a.m., an hour after the time she normally woke. The morning dawn had yet to break the midnight gloom. It must be stormy. She tried to sit up, then groaned and fell back on the pillows. It felt as if someone had scraped the inside of her throat with sandpaper and replaced her bones with water.

Evelyn stumbled to the bathroom and stared with bleary eyes at her mirrored reflection. No doubt about it, she was sick as a dog on her first day of vacation from work. Figured. She brushed her teeth, swallowed two acetaminophen tablets and lay back down. Snuggling under the covers, she remembered the sound of Sweet Mama's voice. It had simply been a touch of the flu combined with missing Sweet Mama so. She didn't feel relieved at her conclusion, but rather, as if she'd lost something all over again. She closed her eyes and allowed herself to slip back into the soft cocoon of sleep.

When the ring of the doorbell cut into her sleep it seemed like mere minutes later. But when she rolled over and stared at the clock, it was almost noon.

"I saw your car in the driveway," Solomon said when Evelyn pulled open the door. "You doing all right?"

Solomon was one of the best things about Mystic Ridge. The mailman seemed ageless; he'd been there for as long as she could remember, always a smile or kind word for anyone who seemed to be in need.

"I could be better, but then again I could be worse," Evelyn replied.

He smiled at her. "Couldn't we all?"

She started to nod, then gasped. Beyond Solomon, the landscape was white, glistening with snow and frost. She couldn't remember the last time that snow covered the ground in Mystic Ridge.

"It's something else, isn't it?" Solomon said. "The town is frozen shut and stopped cold in its tracks. Everything's closed."

"How is it at the hospital?"

"Half the nurses can't get in because of the roads. I hear they're sending around trucks and snowplows to bring them in."

"Oh my goodness. Maybe I should go in." Evelyn started to back away from the door.

"Hold on. You're sick, it's your vacation and it's not like you get off work more than once in a blue moon. They'll be fine at the hospital."

Evelyn sagged against the doorframe. "You're right. But Solomon, this bug couldn't have hit me at a worse time."

"Go on and get out of this chill and I'll go get your packages and bring them in. Pull that door shut now, and settle yourself on the couch." Solomon hurried away to his truck.

She went into the kitchen and put the teakettle on the stove. It had started to whistle when Solomon came in, hidden behind a stack of packages.

"You can drop those under the tree. I'll go through them later. Can you stop for a cup of tea?" Evelyn asked. "I have some Christmas cookies too. They're from Sweet Mama's recipes. I remember how you used to love them."

"I can't resist that offer." Solomon carefully picked a ginger man from the plate she proffered and ate it in two bites. "You sure got Sweet Mama's touch in the kitchen." He looked around. "Yeah, Sweet Mama's spirit is here, as strong and proud as ever."

The hairs crept up on the back on Evelyn's neck. "I know what you mean," she whispered. "Sometimes it seems as if I can still hear her voice."

Solomon shot a glance at her. "Your family's roots are deep in Mystic Ridge's soil. Before Sweet Mama died she said it was about the time to set some wrongs right."

"What are you talking about?"

"Those old stories; your family curse."

"You're talking about the old family legend? That's ridiculous. The curse is just a myth to explain our run of bad luck with men. And how could you set some curse over a hundred and fifty years old right anyway?"

Solomon carefully chose a chocolate cookie and took a sip of tea before answering. "The only way to break any sort of darkness is with the power and light of love. Life is a circle, my dear. What goes around will always come around again. You can catch it if you're at the right time and place. A man cursed your ancestress in hate. Another man, the right one at the right time, can bless you with his love."

A bird trilled loudly and the church clock chimed. Solomon cocked his head. "Sounds like the time is close."

Evelyn shivered. "Solomon, quit it. You're scaring me. That old story doesn't make any sense. It's all confused and I don't believe it anyway."

A sad look covered Solomon's features. "It happened all right. Your ancestress was a house slave. It was a coveted position and one she just gained. She was famous for her cooking, and the cook's position was always fairly secure in the big house. She wouldn't have to worry about being sold or mistreated as long as she cared for others and dished up the food well.

"But she fell in love with a slave from a neighboring plantation. The personal servant of the owner's son, some say he was his brother. They had asked permission to marry and been refused. She became pregnant anyway. They made plans to run North. She was supposed to meet him by the old creek.

"She fretted and worried. She had a secure position and any child she had would be well cared for. If she ran up North she'd be risking it all. Was love worth it? She decided not. She sent her sister with a message that she couldn't meet him. Her sister told him that she didn't love him and offered herself in her sister's place. He spurned Clara's sister and she reported his intentions and whereabouts to his master.

"His master sent the dogs. It stormed that night and the creek was wild and swollen. He let the waters take him rather than return to his plantation as a slave. They say that the last words on his lips were a curse to the women of his lover's family…that they should be ever alone."

"And since then there have been no male children born that survive, no marriages that last, no man that stays or survives. We are a family of women," Evelyn finished.

"But the circle is closing. A change is coming soon." Solomon sat his teacup down and stood. "I got to get on my rounds. You take care of that flu, you hear?"

Evelyn nodded. She shivered again, but it wasn't from the cold.

Evelyn went back to the bed after a generous dose of nighttime cold medication. When the doorbell woke her again, she opened her eyes to the heavy headache of too much sleep. She looked at the clock and gasped. Five-thirty in the evening! She couldn't believe she slept that long.

The doorbell rang again. It wouldn't be her sisters. They all had keys and freely used them. She got up and pulled on her robe.

The bell rang. "Hold on, I'm coming," she yelled and immediately regretted the pain it caused to her sore throat.

She pulled open the door and further words dried on her tongue. The man standing on her doorstep was as handsome as a bronze Greek god or a gilded African prince. He smiled at her. His smile started at the corner of his mobile well-shaped lips and lit up his fire-touched tawny brown eyes. "Evelyn," he said. "It's good to see you after so many years."

Her eyes widened with alarm and she pulled her blue faded chenille bathrobe closer to her body. David Douglas was standing in front of her in the flesh and her hair was standing on end, she didn't have on a speck of makeup, and her sleep-swollen face probably looked as if she'd been through a prizefight.

"May I come in?" he asked.

"Uh, of course." She stepped back from the door. "Please sit down. Excuse me for a moment. I need to get dressed." She fled.

Back in her bedroom she pulled on a pair of jeans and a T-shirt and grabbed a brush and tried to scrape back her hair into a semblance of a ponytail.

She pulled open the bedroom door. What in heaven's name was David doing here? She took a deep breath and walked into the living room.

He was looking at her books. He withdrew a much-read volume from the bookshelves and turned to her. "I love this book. I must have read every single book from this writer at least three times." His thumb caressed the paperback cover lightly.

"Yes, Maya Angelou is one of my favorite authors too."

She hesitated. Asking someone what he was doing in her house could be awkward. "Won't you sit down?" she asked, gesturing toward the couch.

He sat and looked at her, obviously waiting for her to speak. Silence fell as Evelyn searched her mind frantically for the words to say.

"I expected your sisters to be here," David said. "Especially Janet, since she was so insistent that I come for dinner at your place tonight."

Dinner! That was it. She remembered the conversation from last night and her initial relief was followed immediately by alarm. She hadn't cooked a thing all day. She'd completely forgotten about dinner. Every piece of meat in the house was frozen. What was she going to do? She sneezed.

"God bless you."

"Uh, thanks," she said, reaching for a Kleenex. "Excuse me," she said, and blew her nose.

"You've got a cold."

"Yes. I've been in bed all day. And I've got to confess, I completely forgot about dinner."

"I understand. But where are your sisters? After all, technically, they are the ones who invited me."

"I have no idea."

The phone rang and Evelyn reached for it.

"Girl, we slid down an embankment," Deb said as soon as the hello slipped out of Evelyn's mouth. "It's hell out here. The tow guys are going to have to winch out Janet's new car. She's been griping nonstop. She had the nerve to say it all my fault—"

"Are you two all right?" Evelyn interrupted.

"We're fine, but I don't see how we are going to make it over in time for dinner."

"David Douglas is here."

"Better you alone with him than that barracuda Janet. After you feed him be sure and invite him back."

"Deb…"

"I got to go. Here's our ride. See you." Then a click and the sound of a dial tone filled Evelyn's ear.

She slowly set the phone on the cradle. "My sister's car went off the road. They won't be able to make it for dinner."

"They're all right?"

"Deb says they're fine, although Janet's not happy about the damage to her new car."

"I'm sorry about that. And you're not feeling well. Maybe we should all get together another time?" he asked.

"Ummmmm, yes...another time."

He smiled at her and she swallowed hard. The man was so fine. He had the tall lean grace and chiseled good looks she remembered from high school, but his features were overlaid with a fine-polished patina of maturity, and his body radiated pure masculine sexuality.

David got up heavily and walked to the door. When she saw his limp, her heart went out to him. That touch of vulnerability made him even more appealing. "Are you okay?" she asked.

"I'm fine. The cold and damp have made me a little more stiff, but it'll pass."

He picked up his coat that he'd laid over a chair and pulled it on. "It's nice to see you again," he said. "You were one of my favorite people in high school."

She was? She wasn't in his crowd, but rather was simply one of a number of young women who had cast admiring glances his way.

"I hope you feel better," he was saying.

"I'll be fine. Uh, sorry about dinner. I hope you can come back soon."

"Sure. Give me a call." Then he was out the door. Evelyn leaned against the doorjamb, heedless of the frosty air, and watched him make his way to his father's Buick on the curb.

The hole within her heart echoed with something like longing as she watched his lithe body move through the snow. What wouldn't she give for once in her life to have a man like that? Keep dreaming, sister. It wasn't about to happen. Not to a woman like her.

David's car motor revved. Evelyn started to move away from the door and drew it shut. But then his wheels spun in the ice with a sharp whine. He rocked his car forward and back again. Then Evelyn gave a little shriek as his car lurched forward suddenly and slipped past the curb into the gutter.

A moment passed and he slammed the car door behind him. He crunched through the snow back to her door. "Looks like I'm going to be here for a while," he said.

Evelyn nodded and stood aside to let him in.

CHAPTER THREE

David paced as he talked on the phone. His strides were loose and easy instead of nervous or tight. Evelyn imagined she could see his high, rounded buttocks flex through his khakis. She bit her lower lip, filled with a mixture of worry, anticipation and excitement. David Douglas, the finest specimen of man she'd ever laid eyes on in her entire life, was stranded in her house, probably for the night.

He laid the phone down and looked at her. "Seems like you're going to have to put up with me for the night," he said.

She was struck by a paroxysm of coughing and grabbed for a tissue.

David's brow creased as he looked down at her. "You're sick. Stretch out on the couch." She stared at him, confused.

"Now," he said reaching over her and picking up the afghan blanket draped over the back of the sofa. She lay down and he covered her with the blanket, tucking it in around her sides. He was close, too close. He smelled of sandalwood and spicy cloves. She closed her eyes for a moment and his hand grazed her hip.

"I make the best chicken soup in the state," David said.

Her eyes flew open. "What?"

"I make the best chicken soup in the state and I'm going to go and make you some now."

"The chicken's frozen."

"You have a microwave, don't you?"

"Yes, but—" She started to struggle up.

"Please don't move." He gently pushed her back on the couch and handed her the television remote. "Here, watch a little TV. I'll make you some tea and toast to hold you until the soup is done and I'll have some too."

"But—"

"No buts. I know my way around a kitchen. Let me take care of you. It's the least I can do for your having to put up with me all night when you're sick."

His words, "Let me take care of you" dried the protests on her tongue. Evelyn watched mutely as he disappeared into the kitchen. Nobody ever took care of her. It was her job to take care of everyone else.

Evelyn supposed she'd have him sleep in Ashley's old room tonight. She looked at her watch. It was barely six. The evening was young and she was going to spend it with the most eligible bachelor in town. She knew she looked a mess. She raised her head and it started pounding. She gave a little groan and let her head fall back on the pillow.

David walked in with a steaming cup of tea and a plate of hot buttered toast. "It's a good thing I got stranded here. You're far too sick to be alone tonight," he said. He put everything on the coffee table, and disappeared. A moment later he had two plump pillows from her bed. He raised her effortlessly with one hand and put the pillows behind her, plumping them and leaning her back against the fluffy softness. "You rest. I'm going into the kitchen and prepare to show off my stuff."

Evelyn smiled weakly at him and watched him walk away toward her kitchen. Lord, that man looked as good going as he did coming. She turned on the TV and sipped her tea. It was good. He'd sweetened it with honey and added a touch of lemon. The sound of canned laughter on the television soon became annoying and she clicked the TV off and snuggled back into the pillows. It felt both strange and good to hear someone rattling about her kitchen while she relaxed.

David Douglas still had the sweet charm she remembered from high school. He'd been unfailingly kind and usually cheerful. He was also still more than enough in the looks department to send any woman's pulse fluttering. She used to fantasize about him when she was a teenager, along with half the female popula-tion of Mystic Ridge around her age, she was sure. Evelyn's eyes closed and she drifted away...

The smell of greenery and spring air sweet and fragrant with new and tender blooms assailed her nostrils. She was lying under a willow tree, in a soft bed of bruised young leaves and fresh cut hay, a long unbleached muslin dress pushed up around her smooth brown legs.

The leaves parted and there David stood, dressed only in trousers of the same sort of rough material. He went to her and she opened her arms as naturally as a plant turning her face to the sun. He eased his body over hers and his lips touched hers with a passion that was as familiar as it was blazing.

"Clara, my love," he whispered, his voice hoarse. She reached out and caressed his cheek.

"Daniel," she answered.

He kissed her again and their breathing became rushed, their bodies pressing against each other, seeking...

Their hands greedily reached for skin, pulling away clothing, skin against skin. He rained kisses on the curves of her breasts, lower and lower until he encircled her nipple with his tongue. The timeless moans of a woman wanting a man came from her throat. She wanted him, needed him, all of him.

When he moved his hardness across her thighs, she gasped with pleasure. This pleasure with this man felt so right, so perfect, it was why she had been created.

He poised himself above her, his weight on his arms.

"Please, please," she begged, her hips churning. Her feminine emptiness needed and wanted to be filled with this man more than anything in the world.

Her legs grasped his slim hips and he started to move against her.

"Evelyn." Her eyes fluttered open and met Daniel's—no, David's, warm brown eyes. "Evelyn, are you all right? You were gasping…"

"I'm fine," she said, feeling heat under her skin. It matched the warmth of her lingering arousal and the moistness she felt between her thighs. "I was sleeping."

"I've got your soup." He set her food before her on a wooden tray with a flourish. He handed a spoon and napkin and settled back into the recliner with a glass of iced tea and an expectant look.

She could hardly look at him without remembering the vision of him unclothed in her dream, all lean rippling muscles and smooth caramel skin. When had been the last time she'd had a man? She couldn't readily remember, so obviously the experience hadn't been worth remembering. She knew she'd remember a man like David Douglas forever. What had she called him in her dream? Daniel. And what had he called her?

"So how is the soup?"

"It's delicious," she said. It was. The soup was delicately spiced and rich with chunks of chicken, egg noodles, carrots, onion and celery. He hadn't been lying when he said he made good chicken soup.

"Aren't you eating?"

"I'm not hungry. I did my share of tasting in the kitchen. Eating your own food is not nearly the fun of cooking it."

"I know what you mean. Sometimes it seems as if I do most of my eating at the stove too."

"It's good to get a break from your own cooking once in a while." David looked at her closely. "You have a dreamy look yet around the eyes. Were your dreams good?"

She shot a glance at him, alarmed. How could he know?

"Or did you have nightmares?"

She dipped a corner of her toast into her soup and took a sip of the orange juice he'd put beside her plate before answering. "I dreamed of things that were out of my reach."

"Ahhh. I know. Sweet dreams that leave a taste of dissatisfaction with yourself or your life in your mouth."

"I can scarcely imagine you dissatisfied with either," Evelyn said.

David looked away. "A life lived without mistakes and regrets is a life not fully lived."

"Are regrets made lighter through sharing them?" she asked.

He met her eyes. "I don't know. Are they?"

"I've only made one mistake of any significance in my life and it was a doozy. But I can't bring myself to regret it."

"Your daughter."

"Yes, my daughter. What about you?"

"I have two children I hardly ever see. Those are my biggest regrets. Two women whose hearts I failed to hold. Mistakes. When I married, I always had this fantasy of happily-ever-after."

"Doesn't everyone?"

"I suppose." He sighed. "Did you ever marry?"

"No. I've never had the opportunity. I'm pretty busy, you know?"

"Do you have the inclination?"

"Sometimes the idea of the companionship is nice. But then I see some of my acquaintances' marriages and it seems as if I'm not doing too bad. We're a close family, my sisters and I."

"Yes, I remember. They are very different from you."

A wry smile crossed Evelyn's lips. "More attractive, more outgoing, you mean."

"Not necessarily. I find your company very easy, and you know beauty is in the eye of the beholder."

Evelyn took another sip of soup, feeling flustered. "This soup is really good," she repeated.

"One thing about sharing regrets," David said.

"What is that?"

"It might not make the regrets lighter, but it does make the one you shared them with a friend." When he smiled at her, it felt as if the sun broke through the sky on a rainy day.

Evelyn inhaled and exhaled slowly. "I can't eat any more. My appetite…"

David stood to take her plate and touch her fore-head. "You're burning up. You should be in bed."

She couldn't protest. He took her hand and pulled her up from the couch. She felt her hand trembling within his like a small, hot bird as he led her to her bedroom. He turned to her at the door and she thought her heart would stop when his head lowered toward hers. He dropped a friendly kiss on her forehead.

"The linen closet is outside the bathroom. There's bedding in there. You can sleep in Ashley's room," she managed to say.

"Take some aspirin," he said. He turned and left and she closed the door behind him, feeling bemused. She felt as if she was in some sort of fairy tale, stranded alone with this fine man for the night. Just her luck she'd have a raging fever, cough and sniffles. She pulled off her clothes and had just dropped a flannel nightgown over her head when she heard a soft knock on the door.

"Your pillows," David said, holding them out. She took the pillows from him and held them to her chest. "Sweet dreams," he said. Suddenly, his head cocked to one side. "Do you hear that?"

She listened and her eyes widened. There was the faint sound of women singing.

"Have you left on a radio anywhere?" he asked.

"No. I haven't."

He shrugged. "Must have been the wind."

"No, I heard it too. Women singing."

"It probably came from outside." He drew closer to her and she held her breath. "I had a really good time, probably a whole lot better than if things had turned out as planned."

Her heart pounded. "I don't feel as if I've been much of a hostess."

"You've been wonderful." A flash of that crooked smile and he was gone.

There was a sound like a slow, collective exhale after the door closed behind him. Evelyn looked around the room. "The last thing I need is to be haunted. Do you hear me, Sweet Mama?"

"You say something to me?" David called through the door.

"No. I didn't say anything. Good night." Evelyn crawled under the blankets. The smell of spring and freshly cut hay wafted across her face and she sat up in bed. It was the middle of winter in the biggest snow-storm in years. What was going on? She remembered David's cocked head and quizzical expression at the faint sound of women singing. If she was losing her mind, maybe she wasn't losing it alone.

She thought about what Solomon said about the circle of life going around. He had said another man, a man coming at just the right time, would bless her with his love, thus ending the family curse. Was David a part of that circle? Somehow it felt as if they belonged to each other, as unlikely as that seemed. But curses and old family legends were things dreams were made of. Dreams that a man like David really belonged to her were as elusive and unreal as magic.

CHAPTER FOUR

Evelyn opened her eyes to the aroma of coffee. Daniel was here, she thought, filled with a warm glow at the thought of his strong hands and loving heart. Daniel? David. David was here and she didn't know a thing about his strong hands on her body and she likely never would.

Evelyn stood and touched her head. She felt much better. At least the flu bug had been of short duration. Walking to the dresser mirror, she stared at herself and sighed. No, she had no hope of snaring a man like David. Her short black hair, barely long enough to scrape into a ponytail, stood straight up. Her relaxer sorely needed a touch-up, because the naps on the back of her neck were threatening to take over.

Her body was sturdy and plump, not willowy with feminine curves like her sisters. Her skin was the color of Hershey's chocolate, her features distinctly African. Brothers who would turn all the way around when one of her sisters passed wouldn't give her a second glance on the street.

Evelyn Sweet was no one's flavor of choice. That had been just fine with her, seeing all the trifling men her sisters had racked up...until now. David Douglas pulled strings in her heart she didn't even know she had. There seemed to be some sort of indefinable connection between them. Like they knew each other—intimately. She sensed that he felt it too. She remembered her dream of Clara and Daniel. Evelyn and David? The circle turns.

She bit her lower lip and turned away from the mirror. She needed to stop thinking foolishness. She'd have to leave this room to face David sometime. It would be better to do it showered, groomed and dressed rather than sick and in disarray like she'd been yesterday.

Then she heard the shower come on and sank back on the bed. The thought of him in her shower, hot water sluicing over that perfect body…oh my. Then Evelyn shook her head to clear it. Her thoughts hadn't wandered so persistently in those directions since she'd been a teenager. Get a grip, girl.

David turned his face up to the showerhead. The warm water felt good. He'd had a good night's sleep, much better than he thought he'd have in a strange bed. But being here in Evelyn's house felt wholly comfortable to him. Her home was like her, warm, old-fashioned and comforting. He liked her immediately, more so than his usual somewhat guarded reactions to women. She was also quite unlike the type he usually dated. He couldn't imagine dating Evelyn, or any sort of casual relationship with her, really. But he could imagine living with her…waking up next to her every morning of the rest of his life.

He turned off the shower with a quick motion. What was wrong with him? He barely knew the woman. At this stage of the game it was normal to think about what a woman looked like naked or their sweaty, heaving body underneath his own, but domestic bliss? Hardly.

He toweled himself off with a towel and wrapped it around his waist. He needed to shave badly. He remembered seeing a package of disposable razors in the linen closet outside the bathroom. He adjusted the towel and opened the door.

David looked up into the astonished faces of three women. Evelyn's sisters.

Evelyn heard the shower cut off. Keys jangled in the front door a few minutes later and Evelyn sat bolt upright in her bed. Oh Lord, her sisters. You know they'd find a way over at the crack of dawn to find out what the story was with David. She reached for her robe.

"Good morning," she called as she pulled open her bedroom door. Evelyn drew in a breath at the tableau that unfolded in front of her. David stood there, frozen like a bronzed god with only a towel draped around his middle. Her three sister's eyes bugged and their jaws dropped toward the carpet. For some reason the sight satisfied Evelyn. "I'm surprised you're here so early," she said calmly to her sisters.

Her words seemed to unfreeze David. "I'm going—going to get dressed now," he said and fled to the bathroom.

. Evelyn smiled at her sisters and went into the kitchen. She poured herself a cup of coffee. It would probably take a minute or two for her sisters to pick their jaws up off the floor and make it into the kitchen. She started to get cups for them, but then settled back into her chair. They knew where the coffee cups were.

Sure enough, her sisters sailed in, wafting a residue of shock. "So what happened?" Janet demanded. "Why did that man spend the night?"

Beverly chuckled. "It's obvious what happened. It's about time you finally got some, Evelyn."

"I don't believe that for a moment David Douglas is that hard up," Deb snapped.

Evelyn sat her cup of coffee down so hard on the table that it splashed and overflowed. She ignored the spill. "Excuse me, what do you mean, hard up? I see you need reminding that this is my house you're standing in."

Beverly pulled out a chair and sat. "I need a cup of coffee," she said.

"So do I," said Janet.

They both looked toward Evelyn. She didn't move.

Janet frowned, then got up and got herself a coffee mug out of the cabinet and poured herself a cup. "I don't know what's gotten into you," she muttered to Evelyn.

"How about David Douglas?" Beverly cracked.

"I wouldn't believe that until I saw it in action," Janet said.

"Where's my cup of coffee?" Beverly asked Janet.

"Get it yourself."

Deb was still glowering and pouting at Evelyn's retort.

Evelyn chuckled, stood and stretched. "I'm going to shower and dress," she announced. Her walk had a decided bounce to it as she walked out the door.

David entered the kitchen with some trepidation. Evelyn's three sisters sat around the table sipping coffee. From the way the conversation stopped when he walked into the room, he knew they'd been talking about him.

"Hello, everyone. I was wondering if any of you could give me a ride home."

"You're having car problems?" one of the sisters asked. Janet, he thought her name was. He always got them mixed up. They looked so similar, and so different from Evelyn.

"My car slipped in the ice last night. It's stuck."

"Ahhh," said the smallest sister, the youngest one. The syllable was laden with understanding. *So that's why you spent the night with my ugly sister,* she'd said without words.

David felt a surge of protectiveness toward Evelyn. "Yeah. I don't regret it, though. If it wasn't for that I wouldn't have had the opportunity to…get to know Evelyn better." And with those words he strode from the kitchen.

He knocked on Evelyn's bedroom door.

"Come in," she said in her soft voice.

He closed the door behind him. Evelyn stood in front of her dresser mirror, makeup scattered in front of her.

"I'm going to ask one of your sisters for a ride home."

Her face closed like a shutter and she turned and faced the mirror. "Okay."

"How do you feel?" he asked.

"Much better."

"That's good," David said. "I wanted to let you know privately how much I enjoyed our conversation last night."

"It didn't seem like we talked much. I spent most of the evening asleep. But that chicken soup was wonderful. I should be thanking you."

"No thanks needed. Sleep and chicken soup are probably why you feel better today." He paused. "I wanted to also let you know that I'm not interested in your sisters."

Evelyn turned to the mirror and picked up her lipstick. "It would be none of my business if you were."

"I wish you could make it your business. I'd like to see you again."

She turned and faced him, a glint of anger in her eyes. "I don't need your pity, David Douglas."

"You don't have it. You do have my interest, though."

She looked down in confusion and David caught her chin and pulled it out, forcing her eyes to meet his. The door flew open and her three sisters all fell into the room.

"That door latch must be broken," Janet said. "Sorry." Her sisters all backed out of the room and pulled the door shut again.

David and Evelyn looked at each other and simultaneously chuckled.

"Your sisters are a mess," he said.

"Don't you know it. A little shaking up is good for them."

"It's better for you. I sense you need a change in your life, Evelyn Sweet. I sense it with every bone in my body."

Her smile faded and David hated to see it go. Her smile lit up her face and the beauty of her soul radiated from her features. He didn't understand why she didn't consider herself attractive.

"It seems as if I've heard that I need a change from several different people," she said.

David caught her hand. "I think that your change is right here, Evelyn," he said.

CHAPTER FIVE

Evelyn looked out the window at the swirling snowflakes. It would be a white Christmas, the first one in Mystic Ridge in five years or more. The town was frozen, stopped cold, but the houses glowed with holiday lights and activities. Evelyn felt more alive than she had in years. There was a tingling quality there, a breathless anticipation. It had nothing to do with the Christmas season and everything to do with David Douglas.

The ring of the phone interrupted her thoughts.

"Hi, Mom. I just wanted to tell you I'm not going to make it home until Christmas Eve," her daughter, Ashley, said.

Evelyn let her silence reply.

"Travis is having this great party and I've promised Melanie I'd go shopping with her," Ashley continued.

"What about us?" Evelyn asked. *What about me?* She wanted scream the words. She missed Ashley so much sometimes. This growing up and growing apart hurt more than seemed fair.

"I'll be there for Christmas. Knowing you, I know you have all the Christmas arrangements under control and the sisters haven't lifted a finger to help."

"I miss you, Ashley."

"I miss you too, Mom. The best thing about Christmas for me wasn't the presents, but all the stuff we did together, especially the cooking."

"And the tasting," Evelyn added with a chuckle.

"It's just that now, well…my friends are important to me too. I just started dating Travis and he really wants me to be there for him."

"Do you want to ask him here for the holidays?"

"His family would freak if he didn't spend Christmas with them."

"Believe me, I understand. Speaking of—I think I'm going to ask David here for the Christmas Eve dinner."

"They put you up to that? Aunt Deb, I bet."

"No. I've been seeing him the last couple of days."

Silence. Then a shriek. "You're kidding, Mom!"

"Nooooo, I'm not kidding, although I can hardly believe it myself. It seems that he's taken an interest in me."

"You know, I'm not surprised. You know I love my aunts, but you're nicer than all of them put together."

A warm glow filled Evelyn at her daughter's words. "He might not be able to come, but I didn't want you to be surprised in case he shows up."

"You go, Mom. Don't let your sisters put a damper on this. I bet Aunt Deb is having a fit. It's about time you went for the gusto."

"David Douglas might be a little more gusto than I can handle."

"No woman would have any problem handling that. He might be old, but he's fine."

The beep of call waiting broke in. "Hold on, Mom," Ashley said. A second later, she was back. "I gotta go, it's Travis."

"Bye, baby," Evelyn murmured before she hung up. Her daughter was right. It was about time she had a taste of the gusto.

Evelyn touched her hair nervously before she pulled open the door.

David stood there, blindingly handsome in a suit and tie. "You look great," he said.

Evelyn smiled at him and picked up her coat. He took it from her and gently eased it over her shoulders. "I had to make reservations," he said.

"At La Costa?" It was the only decent restaurant in town, but reservations had never been required before.

"Mystic Ridge is full of friends and family this holiday season and it seems as if a lot of people are eating out."

"I've eaten out more these last few days than I've done the past few years," Evelyn said, as they walked down the shoveled driveway to David's car.

"Good. Someone else needs to do the cooking for you once in a while. How are your sisters holding up under the strain?"

They'd discussed her sister's complaints about the lack of dinners at Evelyn's house the last few days.

"They're griping, but I notice that none of them look like they're going hungry."

The maitre d' seated them in an intimate, quiet spot. They ordered their food and Evelyn fingered her wine glass. David looked around. "It's good being home, but I could never live here again."

Evelyn's stomach fluttered and she lifted her wine glass to her lips. "Why not?" she asked.

"I've experienced all this town has to offer. There's too much out there. My heart has moved on."

"I don't think my heart could ever leave Mystic Ridge. It feels as if I'm a tree planted here. My roots are deep," Evelyn said.

"Nothing could persuade you to uproot yourself?" David touched her hand.

Her mouth dried. "I'm afraid I might wither," she whispered.

"Not if you're well cared for."

Evelyn looked away. She had to be reading in the undertones of this conversation. He couldn't possibly mean…It was far too soon.

"How is your father?" she asked.

"Dad is perfectly content. He's dating a widow from church and he's set in his routine. He's happy to see me, but it feels like I've unsettled his routine more than anything."

"So what are your Christmas plans?"

"Dad's going to celebrate Christmas with his lady friend, Gina Brown, and her family. It's the third Christmas he's done so and I understand he's sort of expected. He's looking forward to it. I'm invited of course," David added.

"I'd love to have you join us for our Christmas Eve dinner. Christmas too, if you like," Evelyn murmured.

David's face lit up, and he intertwined his fingers with hers. "I'd like that," he said.

A rush of pure happiness filled Evelyn. Their eyes met and it felt as if the world stopped for a moment. It made no sense. They were so different and almost strangers, but being together felt so right.

"Our family has some Christmas traditions," she said. "On Christmas Eve the kids go over to Bev's and they tell stories and such. The adults go over to Sweet Mama's house and we have Christmas Eve dinner and exchange our gifts. Christmas Day the kids come to Sweet Mama's and open their presents. We generally eat all day and pass out in a stupor sometime near evening."

David chuckled. "Sounds nice. Especially the eating part."

Despite the conversation, Evelyn's attention was focused on her hand in his. Electricity seemed to flow between their fingers.

"I'm looking forward to it," he said and paused. "Evelyn—I wonder…Does it ever seem to you that we've met before?"

Evelyn withdrew her hand, shaken. "All the time."

"Are you thinking about high school?" he said. "I mean it's more than that. Sometimes it feels like we've been together before—like we've had a relationship before."

"Like a dream?" Evelyn whispered.

David frowned and looked away. "No. My dreams are disturbing lately. That's unusual. I've never remembered my dreams before."

"Tell me."

"I dreamed I was drowning in a rush of water. It was terrible. The water filling my lungs, the utter despair, then the blackness."

"My mother and grandmother drowned together."

"I'm sorry."

"We never found out what they were doing by the creek in the rain like that. A flash flood and they were washed away."

David's face was grave and his thumb rotated in the center of her palm.

"It was a long time ago," she continued. "I mentioned it because afterwards, for a long time, I had dreams about drowning. I remember how awful it was."

"You understand. I've only had this dream once, but I remember it as if it actually happened."

"Sweet Mama told me that water in dreams means emotions. She said I was afraid of my emotions and grief overwhelming me."

David nodded. "That's a good explanation," he said and looked away. Evelyn looked at her plate and picked up her fork.

The subject of dreams was an uneasy one.

"The mailman, Solomon, told me something the other day. He was talking about our family legend," she said. The water is deep and you don't know where the currents lead, but jump on in.

"Family legend? That sounds interesting. Tell me about it."

Evelyn shifted with embarrassment. It wasn't easy to tell a man you're intensely attracted to about this particular sort of curse. "A slave from a neighboring plantation had fallen in love with our ancestress. They'd made plans to run north. At the last moment she changed her mind. He ended up drowning in Sorrow Creek and he cursed her with his dying breath." Evelyn paused and took a deep breath.

"What was the curse?" David asked.

"That there would be no men in our family."

"No men? How could that be?"

"We generally only have female children and our marriages don't last long. That is, if we're lucky enough to marry in the first place."

"That does seem like bad luck."

"I think it's just a made-up story to account for our sorry track records with men."

"My family has nothing as romantic as a family legend and a curse."

"It would be our luck to have a curse that's the opposite of all things romantic. Solomon said that maybe our luck will change soon."

"Oh?"

"He said the time is coming where we can be decursed."

"How is that?"

"I'm not sure. Something with men."

"I'd sure hope so."

They both started laughing at the same time. Then the conversation turned to comfortable subjects—the past, mutual acquaintances, her job. Evelyn felt wholly relaxed in his presence. Meant to be.

Afterwards, when they stood at her front door, they turned toward each other. "Do you want to come in for coffee?" Evelyn asked.

"I better not." David's eyes were full of some unfathomable emotion. He bent his head toward her and pulled her close. When his lips touched hers, a spark of electricity traveled through her. His lips were mobile, firm, warm. His arms around her felt so right. *Too right.*

She trembled. She felt him tremble too and he drew away. They looked into each other's eyes and she could see the passion clouding his and she knew it clouded hers. This was unbelievable. *Too fast.*

The emotions between them were like a silent freight train rushing. He touched her cheek, turned wordlessly and walked to his car. They both knew if he came in what would happen. *Too soon.*

The phone was ringing as she entered the house, but she ignored it and let the answering machine pick it up. She dropped her shoes in the middle of the living room floor and headed for her bedroom. She uncharacteristically left her clothes on the bedroom floor. As she brushed her teeth, all she could think of were dreams and magic and David Douglas. Her feelings for him had turned into wildfire, quick and all-consuming.

No, it wasn't like her at all. She was a naturally cautious person, a person unused to and leery of change. She was letting this man sweep her away as if he were a river and she was helpless against the current. With him she wasn't afraid of drowning. She crawled in bed and closed her eyes, welcoming her dreams.

CHAPTER SIX

Clara woke with a start. The morning sky was turning pink already and she could hear the song of birds. She'd overslept again. She'd have to hurry to get breakfast ready. Tillie would have started the preparations, but the family wouldn't be satisfied without her own soft, fluffy white biscuits.

She didn't want to rise from her coarse bedding and straw mattress. Lately she'd felt tired down to the bones. She touched the soft swell of her belly and her eyes widened. Suddenly she knew. A smile curved her lips. A wondrous thing. A perfect thing. She was going to have Daniel's baby. A part of her was a part of the man whom she loved more than life itself. With her position in this house, his child would be safe. They would never sell her child away from her. Ever.

"Evelyn!" Tillie's voice called...

"Evelyn, wake up, girl!" Deb was sitting on the bed, a cigarette dangling from her fingers.

Evelyn sat up in the bed, still disoriented from her dream. "Put that thing out. You know better than to smoke in my house."

"Well, excuse me," Deb said, but she went into the bathroom and dropped the cigarette in the toilet. "I had to have a cig because I waited forever for you to wake up. You were in here snoring like a wild boar—"

"A wild boar?"

"Okay, so you were just breathing heavy. I made a pot of coffee."

"Good. I need a cup." Evelyn pushed the covers away and got up and went into the bathroom. "Pour me one, will you?" she called. "Lots of cream, no sugar."

"When did I start looking like your maid?" Deb answered.

It was too early in the morning for Deb's crap. Evelyn pushed the door open and came out of the bathroom with her jaw tight. But before she could say a word, Deb threw up her hands and said, "All right. I'm going to get you a cup," and switched out of the room muttering about grumpy sisters.

Twenty minutes later, Deb came back into Evelyn's bedroom proffering a mug of coffee. Evelyn took it, went into the living room and turned on the television to the morning news. Deb trailed her and sat on the chair adjacent, nursing her own coffee.

"What happened with you and David last night?" Deb asked, too casually. "I heard you two were seen at La Costa."

"We had a nice meal," Evelyn answered, her attention pointedly on the television.

"What did he say about me?"

Evelyn looked at Deb. "Why do think he said something about you?"

"Well, that's obviously the reason he asked you out. He must be hesitant to ask me out directly—"

Evelyn snorted in a purposeful imitation of a wild boar. "I'm going to get dressed."

"So what did he say about me?"

Evelyn turned slowly to face her sister and put her hand on her hip. "He didn't say a thing about you. He had quite a bit to say to me, though. He'll be over here Christmas Eve."

"He's coming to spend Christmas Eve! He must really want to see me. What shall I wear?"

Evelyn shook her head. "You just don't get it, do you?"

"Get what?"

Evelyn raised her hand and went into her room, shutting the door behind her. *Lord, give me strength,* she thought. Deb worked her last nerve.

At precisely seven on Christmas Eve, Evelyn pulled the door open for David. He was loaded down with an armful of presents wrapped in bright paper. Deb, overdressed in a short, tight red velvet dress, rushed to him, practically knocking Evelyn over.

"David, I've been looking forward to seeing you again," Deb gushed. "Please come in. I hope those all aren't for me?"

David looked bowled over by this torrent of words. "Uh, they're for everybody," he said.

Deb grabbed the presents from his arms and went to the tree with them, shaking each one carefully before she set them under the Christmas tree. Evelyn noticed her frowning as she stuck a small box way in the back.

She left him to the ministrations of her sisters while she went to the kitchen and poured him some hot buttered rum. He looked like he might need some fortification. Dinner was ready to go on the table. She stood inhaling the aroma-laden air. Duck with lemon sauce, wild rice dressing and Virginia ham, greens and cornbread dressing. Cakes, pies and her special home-made candy cane ice cream, and more. She'd been up all night, and it smelled like it would be worth the effort.

Bev came in. "Time to put the food on the table?"

"Yes. Give me a hand."

"All right." Bev moved toward the table. "Deb's got that poor man cornered," she said. "But I think this is one trophy she's not going to be able to put on her mantel. I doubt if she'll take it well," Bev said.

"Me either."

Bev looked at her out of the corners of her eyes as she poured the gravy into the boat. "I hear that you and David might be an item. Deb says it's not possible."

"Last time I checked, I was just as much a woman as her," Evelyn said.

"I didn't mean it like that. It's just that you've never shown much of an interest in men before."

"Things change," Evelyn said as she picked up the platter of the family's traditional Christmas duck and wild rice dressing. She caught the speculative look Bev gave her as she sailed out of the door.

Let them worry and wonder, she thought. She hugged what she and David had shared together to herself like a delicious secret.

Deb sure was showing her tail, Evelyn thought as she savored her last bite of duck in the delicate lemon sauce. She slid a piece of rum cake on her dessert plate. Deb was laughing too loudly in David's face. How did she know that he hated that? There was nothing she could do to check Deb, so she just watched and inwardly shook her head. How did she know that Deb was making David feel uncomfortable? He was behaving with perfect courtesy, showing no evidence of discomfort whatsoever.

Why did she feel she knew this man so well, body and soul? Heaven knew they weren't a perfect match, she a small-town homebody with plain looks, he an exciting, handsome well-traveled man. Her gifts were a flair for cooking and the ability and love of giving. But with her family she had to admit the giving was wearing thin.

"We need some more whipped cream, Evelyn," Janet said.

"You know where the kitchen is," she answered pleasantly, right before she ate a forkful of rum cake. The cake was really good. She knew she'd outdone herself for the entire meal, but no one had expressed appreciation except David.

Maybe she'd done her sisters a disservice by trying so hard to fill Sweet Mama's shoes. They were dissatisfied women. It wasn't because they didn't have enough money or a good man. It was because they weren't grateful enough for what they did have. That was another thing that made her different. If nothing else, she'd always been grateful. Grateful for her health, for the people she had to love and loved her. Not that her life was perfect, but it was good. The Lord had blessed her. She smiled and glanced at David and he met her eyes and smiled back.

Suddenly it was just the two of them celebrating the advent of Christ into the world. Deb broke the spell by clearing her throat loudly. "The kids are expecting us back soon, so we'd better go open our presents. I can't wait to see what David bought me."

Janet rolled her eyes and Evelyn stifled a giggle.

That girl has always been stubborn.

Evelyn's head snapped up. Sweet Mama was whispering in her ear. The hairs on the back of her neck rose and she could feel the goose bumps forming on her arms. Well, if she was losing her mind, she could at least lose it quietly until the holidays were over.

She followed her sisters in the living room where they sat around the Christmas tree like they'd done every Christmas Eve except the last one, the one when Sweet Mama died. Evelyn could scarcely believe that she hadn't thought of her all day until the ghostly whisper in her ear. How could she be losing her mind? She'd never felt more alive and sane in her life.

"Sweet Mama always said a prayer before we started opening our presents," Evelyn said.

Janet sighed and looked away. "It almost feels like she's here." She looked over at David. "Sweet Mama was our great aunt who raised us. She passed away a year ago on Christmas Eve. We missed Christmas last year."

"I know," David said. "I'm sorry."

"Sometimes it does feel as if Sweet Mama's still here in this house," Evelyn said.

"If Sweet Mama was going to haunt anybody, it would be you, Evelyn. You were always her favorite," Bev said. "You took after her while the rest of us took after mother."

Evelyn took a deep breath. "Maybe Sweet Mama hasn't moved on yet. It's as if she's waiting for something."

Bev shivered and looked around.

"Are we going to ever open the presents or do you all just want to talk about Sweet Mama and that depressing Christmas we had last year?" Deb complained.

"Isn't that just like you?" Janet said. "Always thinking of yourself and some presents when the woman who raised us—"

"I'm going to say the prayer in Sweet Mama's stead this year," Evelyn interrupted.

"Go ahead and say the prayer, Evelyn. Sweet Mama would have wanted that," Janet said.

Evelyn closed her eyes and reached out for the Spirit that had been her main comfort this past year.

"Heavenly Father, we praise your Name every day, and especially in this season. Thank you for the precious gift of your blood and the salvation Sweet Savior Lord Jesus has given us. Help us not to forget this true meaning of Christmas. Let us be willing and able to give with the power and spirit with which you pour out your blessings onto us. We thank you for the gift of life, of health and family. We thank You for the love we share…All this in the name of the Father, Son and Spirit, Almighty God."

She stopped. Sweet Mama's strength and love filled her like a wind and a blessing.

"The longest, darkest night of the year is upon us. The circle turns and the time for the choice comes once again. It's the time to set old wrongs right and the time to make the choice. Choose to walk the path of trust, faith, and love rather than fear. May the binding be broken and our blood set free once again."

She heard a gasp and her eyes flew open. All her sisters were staring at her in consternation and even David looked concerned. "What's wrong?" Evelyn asked.

"You were going to say a prayer and you started, but everything changed. Your voice changed," Bev said, looking worried.

"What are you talking about?" Evelyn asked.

"You sounded spooky, girl," Janet said.

Evelyn got to her feet. Fear replaced the warm loving feel of Sweet Mama's presence and memory of the words she spoke flooded her. They weren't her words. "I'm going to my room for a moment. Go ahead and open the presents. I'll be back."

She walked to her room and threw the door closed behind her. She heard Deb explain, "It's hard on her with the anniversary of Sweet's Mama's death."

Evelyn lay on the bed and closed her eyes. "Sweet Mama?" she whispered. There was no answer but the wind blowing against the windows.

She felt someone enter the room and sit on the bed bedside her. Evelyn turned and opened her eyes and looked into David's concerned brown ones.

"I don't know what's happening to me," she said. "Sometimes I wonder if I'm losing my mind."

David gave a tiny shake of his head. "You're not losing your mind. Your sisters say it's grief and stress, but—maybe it's more than that."

"Do you feel something too? There's a strangeness."

David looked away, silent. He handed her a small box. "For you," he said.

She sat up and ripped away the paper, feeling like a child on Christmas morning. It was a black velvet box, the type of box that holds promises. She held it in her fingers, hesitating.

"Go on, open it," David urged.

She lifted the lid, and a pear shaped diamond sparked on a delicate chain. Tears filled her eyes. It was so beautiful.

"I—I can't. It's too much."

"It's not enough." He took the box from her hand and gently put the chain around her neck.

The diamond fell to the cleft of her breast and sparkled near her heart. A promise. David leaned forward and their lips met. Stars swirled around them. Evelyn wrapped her arms around his neck and they cradled each other. This was where she was supposed to be, with this man. She knew him. She wanted him more than life itself.

"Why do we know each other?" she whispered.

"I don't know. I can't understand it, but I do know you. I can't fight what I feel."

"It's crazy. We don't know the details of each other's pasts or anything about each other, really." Evelyn bit her lip. "It's as if I see your soul."

"Like we've known each other in another life," he said.

Evelyn's head snapped up.

David smiled down at her. "You know what? Let's not fight this."

Evelyn smiled back at him. "Let's not."

There was a sharp rap at the door. "Are you two all right in there?" Deb's voice called.

"We're just fine," David answered.

"We should go back out," Evelyn said. "They're probably worried."

When Evelyn came from the room with David following behind her, all eyes went to the glittering diamond at her breast. Janet gasped, Bev's eyebrows raised and Deb frowned.

"Isn't it beautiful?" Evelyn asked.

Apparently her sisters had been struck speechless because nobody answered.

The phone rang and Deb moved to answer it. She listened a moment and put the phone back in the cradle. "That was Ashley. She's wondering where we are. The kids are expecting us. We'd better hurry and open our presents."

"The presents will still be here tomorrow morning," Evelyn said. "Why don't we open ours with the kids?"

"But we've always opened our presents on Christmas Eve," Janet said.

"Maybe it's time for a change," Evelyn said.

"Whatever," Bev said, obviously impatient. "Let's get going, then."

"I'm not going," Evelyn said. She felt in every cell of her body that her place was here with David this night.

The sisters stared at David. Speechless again, they got into their coats.

"Don't come by too early in the morning," Evelyn said. "I think I'm going to sleep in."

Deb looked like she itched to slap her. "Thanks for ruining Christmas," she said.

"Ruin Christmas? I didn't ruin Christmas Eve. Dinner was lovely," Evelyn answered. She felt serene. No negativity could touch her with David at her side.

"Dinner was great," Janet said.

"Sure was," Bev added. "See you tomorrow." She reached out and grabbed Deb's arm, practically dragging her out the door.

"Merry Christmas," David and Evelyn called out to them in unison, standing together in the doorway. All the sisters stood stock-still, turned around and stared at them again. Janet and Bev finally waved back, with Bev keeping a firm hand on Deb's arm.

CHAPTER SEVEN

The sisters gone, David and Evelyn faced each other. It was as if a chasm was between them, wide open and yawning. A chasm full of uncertainty, doubts and possibilities. The possibility of bliss and the possibility of pain that always comes with intimacy. If they jumped there was no returning.

David stepped toward her and Evelyn raised her face to his. Their bodies came together and they soared through the air. They cleared the chasm. There was no stopping them and no going back.

She didn't know how they made it to her bedroom, but their clothes were falling away and her fingers were touching his body, his fingers learning hers. Blazing, urgent heat flared between them that Evelyn had never experienced before nor even knew existed. Time stopped and her world constricted to the aching need to have him inside her.

When he slid himself into her, she gasped with the wonder and rightness of it. Moving within her with a basic and elemental rhythm, he took her to a place where they were no longer flesh, but where their spirits mingled somewhere beyond ecstasy. The song of the stars and the dance of electrons. Magic. That's what it had to be.

Evelyn awoke with David spooned around her, his arm holding her to him, feeling his warm breath on the back of her neck. There had been no self-consciousness as they loved each other for hours with their bodies along with their souls.

It wasn't that she hated her body or had any huge hang-ups about it, but Evelyn knew she didn't quite fit into the norms of beauty. That's the reason she usually felt self-conscious when exposing her body to a man for the first time. But with David it was different. There was no feeling of inadequacy or, what was that term in the song? Unpretty. She knew her body was perfectly right to him. Yin and yang, male and female.

The truth slipped into her consciousness with a rightness that made her draw in a breath. The shape and size of the body was totally irrelevant. The outer changed, failed and eventually died. What was inside was what mattered. She was far more than the size of her hips or the shape of her breasts. Her stretchmarks and slight blemishes were simply a part of her, a natural byproduct of being a woman and human. She knew David didn't see her as any trophy whose cultural physical attractiveness would boost his own esteem. David saw her as the other half of his soul.

David's extreme good looks were a liability because of the way other women reacted, like Deb. David was who he was inside, a man, as perfect and imperfect as any. A man completely unique and forever hers.

He stirred behind her and she felt his lips at the back of her neck. "Merry Christmas."

"Merry Christmas."

He turned her toward him and nestled her into the curve of his hips. She felt his hardness and it aroused an answering moistness within her.

"We've gone so fast. I know we've had to skip some steps of relationship-building, but everything with you has felt so right. Regrets?" David asked in a husky voice.

"How could I regret the most wonderful thing that has ever happened to me?"

He drew her in his arms and they started the day with the sweetest celebration of all.

Evelyn knew it was her family when the doorbell rang at ten that morning although they rang instead of using their key and walking in like they usually did. She'd been bustling around the kitchen in a last-minute rush and David was helping her.

"I'll get the door," David said as Evelyn bent to pull a sheet of cookies from the oven.

She started to say no, thinking about her sisters' reaction when he answered the door, but then she decided to let him go ahead. They were going to have to get used to David being a part of her life. Then she wondered why was she so certain that was so?

She soon heard the shrieks of excitement of her nieces as they spied their presents under the tree. But she didn't hear the raised voices of her sisters like she usually did when they first came into the house. They were probably in shock to see David still there. Probably, shoot. The odds were one hundred per cent that they were tripping. He might be out there performing CPR. She'd better go rescue the man. Evelyn wiped her hands on her apron and started to hang it on the hook.

Baby, it's only begun. The circle turns and the choice comes.

Evelyn froze. "Sweet Mama?"

The circle turns and the choice comes.

Terror rushed in on her. This was not her imagination and she wasn't losing her mind. This was Sweet Mama. That was the only reason she was still standing in the state of Maryland, much less the room. Sweet Mama, dead or alive, would never hurt her. There had never been anything but love between them and it had to have survived the grave.

"Evelyn?" Bev called as she walked into the kitchen. She stopped at the sight of her sister. "What's wrong with you? You look like you've seen a ghost."

"No. I've just heard one."

"What?"

Evelyn turned to her sister. "Sweet Mama is haunting me."

"Girl, that man has made you lose your marbles. Not to say I don't blame you. If he looked twice at me, I'd toss some marbles his way too—"

"Bev, I'm serious."

The expression on Bev's face changed to one of fear. "I know," she said.

"You know?" echoed Evelyn, hardly believing her ears.

Bev looked around the room and wrapped her arms around herself as if warding off a chill. "I've felt something every time I've walked into this house the past few weeks."

A mixture of fear and relief filled Evelyn. She was right about not being crazy. Someone else had felt it too. "What's been happening?" Evelyn asked.

"I can't describe it easily. It's like walking into a dream. And there's cold spots in the house."

"Cold spots like what?"

"Like when you walk in a refrigerator. Also it feels as if someone is watching me whenever I'm alone in this house, even in the bathroom. You know that feeling?"

"You've discussed it with Janet and Deb?"

"No. We've never talked about it, but I think they know too."

"I hear Sweet Mama's voice," Evelyn said.

Bev drew in a breath. "What does she say?"

"It doesn't make a lot of sense. She talks about circles and choices."

"What are you going to do? Should we get an exorcist or something?"

"Do you really think Sweet Mama could be exorcised from anywhere if she didn't want to go?"

Bev shook her head. "Uh-uh. But it's Christmas. Maybe we should take everything over to my place. You can stay over there for a while. Solomon would know what to do, but it's Christmas and we can't call him to come over," Bev continued.

"Yes, Solomon knows. He's the one who talked about circles for the first time. He talked about the old family legend."

"The curse," Bev whispered.

"Yes, the curse."

"Solomon will know what to do."

"I got the feeling that he thinks everything is as it should be. There's something that he feels I'm supposed to do," Evelyn said.

They stood together silently for a while, each with their own thoughts.

"We've lived with Sweet Mama all out lives," Evelyn said. "What's the big deal? Let's invite her out for Christmas. Sweet Mama?" Evelyn called.

Bev looked as if she was going to have a stroke. But there was no answer but silence.

"What are you doing? Why are you calling for Sweet Mama?" Janet asked, coming into the kitchen.

Bev and Evelyn looked at each other. "She's here," Evelyn finally said.

"Please. Aren't you two going to come out and see the kids unwrap their presents? And Evelyn, let me help you get the food out on the table." Janet grabbed a pot.

"Wait," Evelyn said, but Janet was already gone.

"See, she couldn't wait to get out of this kitchen," Bev said.

"I needed to put that in a bowl," Evelyn murmured and followed Janet out the door. Christmas was here and now and so was David. They could worry about ghosts later.

CHAPTER EIGHT

Evelyn sat alone in her house and stared out her window at the dark, icy landscape of Mystic Ridge. The Christmas lights and tinsel suddenly looked more garish than festive as soon as the day was over. Still, that view was far better than turning around and looking at her house. The house was a wreck with remnants of the Christmas celebration and dirty dishes scattered everywhere. But it was always like that after Christmas passed. Usually at this time she was busy washing up dishes and straightening up the messes.

This Christmas was totally different. Everything had changed. She was looking out of her window waiting for the man she loved to return to her. She was also waiting for something else. Sweet Mama. Ever since Bev and she discussed the reality of Sweet Mama's lingering spirit, there had been emptiness. No hairs rising along her arms, no cold areas in the room, no ghostly whispers. It felt as if Sweet Mama had gone at the moment of acknowledgement. That made Evelyn feel bereft instead of relieved. Sweet Mama's shadow was better than no Sweet Mama at all.

Tears burned her eyes. Emotions she hardly knew she had tumbled and churned within her. How could she be sad with so much new joy? She heard a car door slam and looked up. There he was, David. The sudden warmth of love flooded her with happiness.

He came in and hung his coat on the rack, then turned to her. He kissed her forehead, then raised her chin and looked into her eyes. "Tired?" he asked.

"No. I was just thinking. Can we talk?"

David sat on the couch next to her. "Sure we can talk. I guess there's a lot to talk about."

He had no idea how much, Evelyn thought. "Let me go get us some coffee first. Do you want anything to eat?"

David groaned. "I feel like I've eaten enough the past two days to feed a third world country for a week."

Evelyn grinned, and went to put on the pot of coffee. She took the time to organize what she wanted to tell him.

Setting the cup of coffee on the coffee table in front of him, she nestled next to the arm of the sofa and pulled her legs up beneath her.

"Do you believe in ghosts?" she asked.

David's eyes shot up. "Not really, since I've never met one before." He reached for his cup. "I thought when you said you wanted to talk it would be about us."

"Why would I want to talk about us?"

"Why?" David looked nonplussed. "Why? Because we've known each other a whole week and we have this amazing connection. We've made love. Notice I said made love, not had sex. And we need to be together."

"I agree completely. So what is there to talk about?"

"You don't know a thing about me, for one."

"I know who you are."

"Evelyn. Most women want to talk any relationship to death. What's up with you?"

"I'm not most women. If what you say about us is right, we have plenty of time to talk anyway, don't we? I want to tell you about being haunted by Sweet Mama."

David sat back with a strange look in his eye. "This is the first time in my life I've heard 'can we talk?' from a woman and not been embroiled in some emotional relationship dissection for at least three hours," he muttered.

"Give us time, hon. But pay attention. I want to tell you about Sweet Mama's ghost and what Solomon said."

"I'm all ears."

"I've been hearing Sweet Mama's voice the last week. At first I talked myself into thinking it was a dream or stress, but then I heard her this morning in the kitchen. She said something to me twice, David. It was no dream."

He studied her for a moment. "I suppose I can deal with it if you're somewhat eccentric." He started to reach for her, lust in his eyes.

"C'mon, I'm serious. And you know I'm not crazy. Bev said she felt Sweet Mama's presence too, and Janet about jumped out of her skin when I mentioned Sweet Mama's ghost."

"Ummm. I can't really buy the ghost thing, Evelyn. If there was such a thing as ghosts, we'd hardly be able to turn around without bumping into some dead person. Why would Sweet Mama want to hang around here instead of going on to her heavenly reward anyway?"

"I think there is something for me to do. It involves the family curse and it involves you."

"And what is that?"

"I don't know yet."

David had inched closer and closer until he was a mere inch from her. He dipped his head and kissed the hollow of her throat. He worked his way up her chin with tiny kisses.

"Were you listening to me?"

"Every word. I thought you were done."

He covered her lips with her own. When he raised her head, she looked into his brown eyes. "I guess I am done after all," Evelyn whispered, and reached for him again.

Much later, they lay together, legs and bedding tangled, satiated from their loving. "I've been married twice and it's never been like this," David said. He turned to his side and traced the line of Evelyn's breast.

"What was it like?"

"I married too young the first time."

"You two weren't right for each other?"

"More like I was too young to know how to build the relationship we needed. I was concentrating on my vision of what I wanted our family to be, working hard, trying to get ahead. Several years and two children later we looked at each other over the dining room table and realized we were two strangers who didn't like each other all that well."

"Ouch," Evelyn said.

"The divorce was amiable, but expensive."

"You married again."

"I lived with her for five years before we married. A German woman. Right before I had the car accident, it was pretty much over anyway. It had been a practical relationship that turned into a habit that had pretty much run its course."

"Have you ever been in love with a woman?"

"Before? It depends on how you define love. I've cared, I've committed, but I've never felt I belonged there."

A moment passed in silence. "Why did you never marry?" he asked.

"No one asked me to. My experience with men has been rather limited here in Mystic Ridge. I never thought I'd ever find…"

"Love. Until now," David whispered.

He'd said it. Evelyn turned to him, and touched his cheek. "Until now," she echoed.

"What is happening to us? I've never been an impulsive sort of man, especially in relationships of this sort."

"It's meant to be, I think."

"I think so too. When we leave Mystic Ridge…"

"Leave Mystic Ridge? Why do we have to leave Mystic Ridge?" Evelyn asked.

"My new job starts in a few weeks. It's in San Francisco. You'll love it there. It's the most beautiful city in the world."

"I can't leave Mystic Ridge."

"Why can't you?"

Evelyn sat up against the headboard. "I just can't. This is the soil I was raised in, my roots. Why can't you stay? The cost of living is low and almost any business here would be happy to hire you."

"I can't stay here. I've made a commitment to the position in San Francisco, and furthermore, it's a job I really want in a place where I want to be."

"I thought you said there was an 'us'."

"There is. If there was any good reason why you couldn't leave Mystic Ridge, I'd have to reconsider my plans."

"I just gave you a very good reason that I can't leave. So are you are going to reconsider?"

David sighed. "We need to talk about it more. Is it that you're afraid of leaving without any formal commitment to me? If so we can—"

"That's not it. It feels as if we have a bond together deeper than any papers. You're right. We need to talk about it more when we're not so tired."

They straightened the covers and settled down in each other's arms. Evelyn wasn't worried; she knew deep in her bones that David's place was with her in Mystic Ridge.

Two weeks later, Evelyn opened the door for the realtor. "This area is in high demand and I can see you've kept things up," the plump red-haired woman said as she moved through the door. "It'll probably go fast."

The realtor thrust a sheaf of papers into Evelyn's hands. "Here's a checklist, and there's that other list of things that need to be done within the week."

Evelyn stared at the list of cosmetic things to do to the house. Her heart sank as the idea of leaving Mystic Ridge forever moved further toward a reality.

The realtor stood in the middle of the living room and turned three-hundred-and-sixty degrees. "Yes, it'll go fast," she repeated. "You must be the luckiest woman in the country, no, the world." The woman smiled at Evelyn. "What wouldn't I give to have a man like David Douglas come into town, sweep me off my feet and take me away to glamorous San Francisco. Why, it's like a fairy tale."

"I'm truly blessed," Evelyn agreed readily.

But later, after she closed the door behind the realtor, she felt a sense of dissatisfaction. She and David had discussed it and she had to agree, it made more sense for her to go to San Francisco with him. He had a job that he'd been wanting for years and she could work as an RN anywhere. She had no family ties that couldn't be maintained long distance. Her sisters were adults and her daughter was grown and living her own life.

But still it felt like leaving Mystic Ridge was akin to tearing out her heart. Evelyn sank on the sofa. She almost wished she had continued to hear the otherworldly whispers from Sweet Mama and to have strange dreams. She so needed someone to confide in, and failing that, to distract her. Her sisters had been stunned to hear the news, to make an understatement.

She had not spent much time with them the past couple of weeks because of David. That part felt healthy. With perspective she could see that her constant doing for them had actually done none of them much good, including herself.

She'd started to confide her reluctance to leave Mystic Ridge to Bev. Bev promptly responded that if Evelyn didn't go with that man, she was going to personally beat her ass and haul her off to the State

Hospital afterwards because it would be clear that she'd lost her mind.

Evelyn smiled at the memory. But still, it was crazy, running off with a man she'd only known for a few weeks, soul mates or not. No, that wasn't true. Following David anywhere, any way and any time wouldn't be crazy. He was just as much a part of her as her heart.

Then why the anxiety? Was it simply because she'd grown up here and had never lived anywhere else? Her entire family had been raised on this soil for generations. She'd built a life and security for herself here in Mystic Ridge.

But she knew it was more than that, way more. It didn't have to do with David or Mystic Ridge or her past as much as it had to do with her own fear. She was afraid. So very afraid. She was not a person who took to change easily. And this was almost more than she could handle. She was leaving everything she'd known all her life and jumping into the unknown.

Don't worry so. You made the right choice, baby.

CHAPTER NINE

Clara and Daniel lay wrapped in each other's arms after their lovemaking. The drooping arms of the weeping willow shielded and shaded them. Daniel had covered the ground with soft pine needles, grasses, and crushed clover that gave off a sweet fragrance. It was their own place, their secret room where they escaped to whenever they could.

"I have something to tell you," Clara said.

Daniel propped himself on his elbow and tickled her nose with a soft brushy stalk of grass. "And what is that?"

"I'm going to have a baby."

He didn't fill the silence, but sat upright, looking off into the gently waving green willow walls instead of at her.

"I thought you'd be happy," she said. She didn't quite know what to make of his reaction. She knew with every particle of her body that he loved her, so she'd assumed he'd be thrilled to hear about the child.

He reached out and touched her hand. "It's not that I regret any child of ours. It's that...I vowed to myself that when I had a child, he would not be born into slavery."

Clara sat up beside them and wrapped her arms around her knees. "How would that be? Our stations are what they are. The only thing we can do is accept—"

"It is not the only thing we can do," he said, his dark face was fierce and intense. Clara felt a fear that iced her soul. Black men who showed that sort of anger didn't live long. Black men with Daniel's intelligence and strength who didn't carefully tread the paths set out for them lived even shorter lives—no matter how valuable they were.

"We can run, Clara. We can run. I know a way, a special way called the slave's railroad. We can go North. We can be free, Clara. We can live our own lives. Our own lives, can you imagine? And we can give our children lives of their own too."

Her fear intensified. "What if they catch you? They nearly always do. They kill you for sure, but only after they torture you for their sport and for an example to the other slaves."

"I don't believe my owner would do that. He is my brother."

"When have they ever cared about that? He would laugh as he burned you alive."

"I know this way will be safe. I know of people who will help us. How else could I ask you to join me in this risk?"

She saw by the tilt of his jaw that he had made up his mind and she wanted to scream and cry and rip out her hair. How could she ever live without her Daniel? How could she leave the safety and security she had as the cook for the family who owned her for the unknown North and the similarly unknown promise of freedom?

Evelyn woke like a crack across a mirror and sat straight up in the bed with a strangled groan in her throat.

"What's wrong?" David asked her, his voice blurry with sleep, but alarmed.

"I had a nightmare." She lay back down. "Sorry I woke you."

"Are you sure you're all right? It sounded pretty bad."

"I've had it before. Not the same dream, but the same people. You and me." She paused and picked at the bedding nervously.

"Go on," David said. "It might help to talk about it."

"It's back in slave times. We're lovers."

"I hope that wasn't part of the nightmare."

Evelyn smiled at him. "No. Your name is Daniel and mine is Clara. You want to run North and I'm terrified." David became very still, too still.

"David?"

"Maybe we both learned about those people in school. We had a lot of classes together," he said.

"What are you talking about?"

"I've dreamed about Clara and Daniel too."

"Oh, my God."

"It's a coincidence. Like I said, we've probably both heard of them."

"How could it be a coincidence? It doesn't make sense. What do you think it means?"

"I don't know."

"We should talk to Solomon . ."

"I don't want to talk about it any more." David's voice was sharp and strained, so uncharacteristic of him that Evelyn stared at him.

"I'm sorry, but let's just drop it." He turned on his side, his back facing her. "I'm going back to sleep."

Evelyn let herself into the dark house, loaded down with presents from her going away party at work.

"Surprise!" she heard voices scream and screamed right back at them in shock. Lights clicked on and her sisters and a few of her closest friends stood there dressed in nightgowns, pajamas and lingerie.

"What's going on?" Evelyn asked. She didn't know if she really wanted to hear the answer.

"You didn't think we were going to let you get out of here without a bridal shower, did you?" Janet said.

"We forgive you for planning to elope and get married on some South Pacific cruise, but we deserve our bachelorette party," Bev added.

"So get on your pajamas and let's swing," said Toni, a good friend since high school.

"Uh, why pajamas?" Evelyn asked.

"Because it's a pajama party, silly. Hurry up, now, before the strippers get here."

More than a few hours and several drinks later, she'd lost count, Evelyn waved goodbye to Toni, who'd kept changing her lingerie. Toni had progressed through flannel to Victoria's Secret and finally to Frederick's of Hollywood. Toni waved happily back to Evelyn from over the stripper's muscular shoulder as he carried her out the door.

Evelyn collapsed on the couch amidst her sisters. "Thank you all. I had a great time."

"So did we, sis," Bev said. "We're going to miss you."

"You guys are so great."

"Yep, sis, you're breaking up a great team."

Evelyn grabbed a throw pillow from behind her and buried her face in it, her shoulders heaving.

"What's wrong?" asked Deb.

"I can't stand it. I can't do it. I can't, I just can't. I'm not going to leave you guys," Evelyn said through her sobs.

Janet, Bev and Deb looked at each other over Evelyn's heaving shoulders. "I think it was that Long Island Iced Tea," Janet said. "All those liquors mixed up. Why did you give that to her, Deb?"

"It was in the spirit of celebration," Deb answered. "You know Evelyn didn't know how potent that stuff was. She can't hold her liquor."

"I can too," Evelyn's resentful, muffled voice came from the pillow.

"Stop sitting there yakking and help me get her to bed," Bev said. "You know Evelyn is going to be mad when she wakes up with a hangover in the morning."

"Lord, I don't think she's ever hardly drunk mixed drinks before, she usually sticks to wine."

"Stop talking about me like I ain't here," Evelyn bawled from the pillow.

"C'mon. Get up and help me with her," Bev said.

It was far too soon for her to feel the quickening movements of her babe within her. Clara laid her hands on the slight swell of her belly. She walked to the stool, sank down and buried her face in her hands.

The plans were in place and the time set for Daniel and her to go. The secret burned within her. She would not be able to tell her sisters good-bye or how to reach her. The slightest suspicion, and that slave would be tortured until they revealed what they knew. Even so, they would certainly whip her sisters.

She imagined she heard the whistle of the whip through the air and the screams of her sisters. The ripped flesh and dripping blood. That was nothing compared to what they would do to Daniel if they were caught. What they would do to her and her unborn baby.

Silas had run from the farm a few years ago. It was said that he had got the crazy notion to go up North, get a job and save enough money to buy his family. Silas had been the best blacksmith within three counties and maybe he could have done it. They caught him three days later. They tore out his entrails while he was still living and let the dogs eat them while he dangled from the cottonwood tree where they'd hung him. Silas' white skull still hung in the cottonwood tree as a reminder. They trained no other slaves in any craft or skill after that.

Her fear built within her until she could taste it bitter as bile in her mouth. She couldn't go with Daniel. She wouldn't let him go either. They were valuable livestock. If they did their work and caused no trouble, they and their children would be safe. Freedom was nothing but a dream. Getting up to breathe yet another day, that's what mattered, wasn't it?

Mary walked into the kitchen. "What's wrong with you?" she asked.

Clara straightened and dried her eyes. "You must do something for me. Go to the Bushes. You can take those eggs over there and say they are a gift from the mistress. It's a matter of life and death, Mary. Tell Daniel that—that I can't go with him tonight. I cannot. Tell him to wait for the time until we can meet again."

"Go with him?" Mary asked. "Go with him where?" Clara shook her head. Mary studied her sister's tear-swollen face. "You were going to run," she breathed.

"Just go, Mary, go now. Please."

Mary started to speak, but at another pleading look from Clara, she turned and hurried out of the room.

David chewed his knuckle. He'd woken up from another dream of the dogs and the rushing waters…A dream sharper and more real than a memory. His dreams had never disturbed him as they did now and he'd never remembered them with such clarity. What should he do about it? Therapy? He rebelled against that thought because he was happier now than he'd once dreamed possible.

His love for Evelyn fit him like a buttery leather glove, comfortable and natural. He didn't know what he would have done if she hadn't agreed to go to San Francisco with him. He tried to empathize with her at the loss she felt at giving up familiar Mystic Ridge, but it was hard. He got excited at the thought of what he could show her in the world beyond this town. What they would experience together. He couldn't have picked a better woman to have by his side and grow old with. Certainly they'd travel the world.

He rolled out of bed. It was one of the few nights in the past weeks he'd slept without Evelyn and already he didn't like it. Her sisters were giving Evelyn a wedding shower and they said they might be a little late. He had some things to finish up in preparation for their move.

He heard the doorbell ring and almost groaned. Not before he had a cup of coffee. These dreams were sapping his usual morning energy. He pulled on a pair of jeans and a T-shirt over his head and went to answer the door. He blinked twice when he saw Evelyn's sister Deb there. "May I come in?" she asked.

"Are you here for Dad? He's already left for work." David was unable to fathom what she would want with him.

Deb walked past him into the living room. "I'm not here to see your father. I'm here to see you."

CHAPTER TEN

Something must have crawled down her throat and died in her stomach last night, Evelyn decided. That was the only thing that could account for the misery she was presently experiencing. She groaned and rose up from the bed, squinting her eyes against the pain pounding in her head.

Stumbling to the bathroom, she swallowed three extra-strength acetaminophen. She started to close the medicine cabinet, reconsidered, and took three ibuprofen also. Lurching back to her bed, she closed her eyes. Sleep was unthinkable, but she could lie perfectly still for the twenty or so minutes for the drugs to kick in.

Exactly thirty minutes later, she opened her eyes. She threw back the covers, stood and stretched. Much better. She started to reach for the phone to call David.

The river will churn as the circle closes. Go to him now.

"Sweet Mama? Why are you here?"

For this. Go to him. Remember the choice you've made for trust and love. Remember that fear is the enemy.

"What's up, Deb?" David asked. "Please sit down."

"It's about Evelyn. I want to talk to you."

"Sure. But let me get some coffee first. Want a cup?"

"That would be great," Deb said.

He went in the kitchen and poured two cups, wondering again what Deb had to talk to him about. Whatever it was, he hoped it was quick. He had a ton of stuff to do today. "Want cream or sugar?" he called.

"No. Black will be fine."

He handed her the cup and saucer and sat in an adjacent chair. "So what can I do for you?" he asked.

"It's about Evelyn."

"Oh."

"What happened last night terribly concerned me." David put down the cup and listened.

Deb took a sip. He noticed she seemed a little nervous. "Evelyn was crying and carrying on so. She said that she really didn't want to leave Mystic Ridge. That she felt you were forcing her to leave everything she loved."

David picked up his cup again. "Hmmmm," he said.

"I'm worried sick about her, David. You know she was recently hearing voices. If she puts herself under the kind of stress that I think will happen if she leaves Mystic Ridge, well, I don't know what she'll do."

"Hmmmm."

"What do you think we should do?"

David drained his cup of coffee and stood to get another one. He poured himself a cup and added a dollop of cream. No need to offer Evelyn's sister a refill.

When he returned to the living room Deb was perched on the edge of the couch.

"What do you think we should do?" she repeated. David shrugged.

Deb waited.

"Aren't you going to say something?" she finally asked.

"No."

"Aren't you concerned about Evelyn'?"

"Very concerned."

"So why aren't you saying anything?"

"I was waiting for you to tell me something that made a lick of sense." He stood again. "Since you haven't done so, I have a lot to do today. I'll see you to the door."

Deb's face crumpled and she set her coffee cup carefully on the coffee table. "I just wanted you to see my sister for what she is."

"All you showed me was what you are." He walked to the door and pulled it open. Evelyn was standing there, and she stepped in past him and rushed straight to Deb.

The boy ran up to Daniel while he rubbed the horse down in the stable. "There's a woman here to see you waiting on the rock in the field. She says it's important."

He straightened and wiped his hands on his rough trousers. When he got out to where she sat at the edge of the field, he saw it was Clara's sister, Mary. Disappointment filled him. He had hoped it would be Clara.

"How can I help you, Mary?" he asked.

She looked around furtively and his heart sank. Clara couldn't have told her their plans.

"I have a message from Clara," she said.

He waited.

"She realizes she made a mistake. She no longer loves you, Daniel. She is not going to run with you tonight."

A beat of time passed.

"You lie," he said.

"She will not be meeting you tonight, you will see."

Daniel could say nothing. He felt as if a giant had hit him in the stomach. Since Clara had told her sister of their plans…it might be true. He could not believe that Clara would put them in such danger by entrusting such a thing to this woman.

"But I will meet you in her stead," Mary said. She moved close to him. "I have wanted you for a long time. I'll go North with you since she no longer cares for you. You're too good for the likes of my sister."

His eyes narrowed. "No. I'm too good for the likes of you."

"What did you say?"

"You heard me. I would not have you."

She gasped in disbelief. "But I'm far more beautiful than Clara."

Pity filled him. "You've always believed that, but you're wrong. Clara's beauty outshines yours like the sun to a sputtering candle."

"You have no idea how much I've wanted you," she said, obviously not able to hear the meaning of his words. She reached out for him and he stepped away.

Mary stumbled.

"I do not want you, woman. Go," Daniel said. Her face turned into a mask of fury.

"She told me herself that she hates you. That you were crazy thinking she would run North with you," Mary spat.

"I know Clara would never forsake me." With those words he turned and walked away.

Deb gasped when she saw Evelyn bearing down on her. David wheeled in surprise, and rushed to follow. But all Evelyn did was to grasp Deb's hand tightly.

Then she held out her hand to David. "Quickly. Take my hand. The circle closes."

He caught her hand and there was a cracking in the very air of the room, shattering like glass, breaking into a million pieces. He thought he heard Deb scream. Then suddenly he was thrust into some cold and wet darkness.

Daniel crouched under a tree to provide him some shelter against the pouring rain. He had waited hours for

Clara. The sky was lightening to gray in the east. He was numb and cold inside and out. His Clara hadn't shown up, just as Mary said.

His tears mixed with the rain and he didn't wipe them away. He was man enough to cry. He stared toward the rushing, swollen waters of Sorrow Creek, trying to decide what to do. That was when he heard the baying of the hounds. He knew instantly they were after him. There was no way his owner would have set the hounds after him for one's night absence unless he had been tipped to the fact that Daniel had run away. Mary, he thought, with his teeth grinding. May that wench roast in hell.

The sound of the hounds came closer and he did all that he could do. He ran.

CHAPTER ELEVEN

Daniel's breath ripped through his chest like sharp knives. His muscles were screaming with every step. He wouldn't be able to run for much longer, and the dogs were gaining on him. Daniel looked toward the creek, now a raging torrent of muddy brown water after the hard rains. The snarl of a dog echoed behind him, and he knew he could hesitate no longer. He used his last burst of energy to sprint toward the flooded creek. Possibly it would carry him along to a place where the dogs would lose his scent on the other side.

He threw himself into the boiling rush of dark water and within a few seconds knew he was lost. The raging waters were too much for him. They wrestled and worried him, finally pulling him under. Daniel stopped struggling and let the new river take him home. His last thought was of Clara. Such a love as they had surely could never pass away…

Clara felt as if she was going to lose her mind. She'd been waiting all night for Mary to return. Clara had watched her sister Tillie sleep, wake and start a fire with her usual cheerful unconcern. Clara envied her.

She stood to leave for the neighboring farm where Daniel lived, no matter the trouble it would cost her. Then her hand flew to her mouth as she saw Mary stumble into the cabin. Tillie gasped. Her sister was disheveled and wet, but it was more than that. It was the expression on her face. Anguish, regret, and fear mixed all together. Mary wasn't one given to strong emotion.

"What happened to you?" Tillie cried.

"Let me talk to Mary alone," Clara said. "Tillie, please leave us."

"But it's raining outside!"

"Go stay in the barn a while. I need you to leave us." Something in Clara's voice made Tillie gather her skirts and hurry out the door.

Mary sank to floor in front of the fire and Clara waited until she heard Tillie's footsteps fade away.

"Tell me what happened."

Mary said nothing but continued to stare into the fire.

Clara walked around and crouched down. She looked into Mary's eyes and Mary looked away. "What did Daniel have to say?"

When Mary didn't answer, Clara pulled her hand back and slapped it with all the force she could muster across Mary's cheek. "Tell me what happened to him," she screamed, her fear turning to panic and her breath coming in deep, fast gasps. She could see it in Mary's eyes...She could see the worst.

"They set the dogs on him."

Clara doubled in pain, a moan like a wounded animal coming from her throat. A black mountain of despair crashed down on her and she didn't think she could survive the impact.

Tillie rushed in and ran to Clara. Mary turned her face away and stared back into the fire.

A crack like thunder and they were in a room dressed in strange clothes and holding tight to each other's hands. Mary, Daniel and Clara stared at each other in fear and alarm.

Evelyn. She was Evelyn, not Clara. But she was and had always been Clara too. They were Deb, David and Evelyn in another world and another life. She saw similar knowledge cross their faces and Deb's mouth opened in a scream and David pulled back in horror. Evelyn held on to Deb's hands as tightly as she could despite the struggle. *The circle still closes.* She held on to Deb with every bit of strength she had as the world shattered around them.

Clara ran through the muddy field through the pouring rain lit with the brackish light of dawn. She ran toward her love, toward Daniel and the place she'd promised to meet him. She heard hounds baying in the far distance and stumbled and fell. She lay face down while her fingers dug in the mud in anguish and pain. She knew, felt it in her heart. He was gone. Gone.

It wasn't until the rain had stopped, the sun had risen higher in the sky when a boy from the farm where Daniel had lived found her face down in the field. He touched her shoulder and she lifted her head a little. The boy screamed and jumped back. "I thought you was dead," he said.

"I only feel that way," Clara answered. Her voice coming raw and husky from her throat. She struggled to sit up and finally righted herself.

The little boy peered at her. "Aren't you the cook-lady from over yonder?" He pointed.

"That I am."

"I've seen you before. I'm the houseboy. I saw your sister yesterday in the stables. She was looking for your man." The boy's face clouded. "I'm sorry," he whispered, and looked down.

"What happened to Daniel?" she whispered.

"The dogs chased him into the creek during the flood. They found his body a mile downstream."

So it was true. Daniel was dead. Clara closed her eyes in agony. She'd known it was so, but still she'd held on to that little flame of hope.

"You look so sad. So why did your sister tell them that Daniel was going to run? Everybody wants to know that."

Clara stared at the boy.

Clara stirred the stew with loving attention. She ladled three bowls. One for her, one for Tillie, and one *for Mary. She gave Mary's bowl an extra stir to hide the extra seasoning.*

They ate in silence, not an unaccustomed thing lately. Clara's new silence was attributed to her grief. She left her food untouched. They also mistook her lack of appetite. Clara grieved, but hatred burned within her also.

When her sisters finished eating, she took their bowls for cleaning in silence.

It wasn't until later that night when Mary's stomach cramps started. An hour later she was screaming and sweating in agony. By daybreak, she was dead.

Everyone immediately knew that Clara had poisoned her own sister. Not that the evil wench didn't deserve it, but still she was valuable property.

Clara would have to be punished. Shame to have to whip her in her delicate state, but it had to be done.

They strung her up on the cottonwood, and the overseer flexed the whip and then sent it whistling through the air to rip through the brown skin of Clara's back again and again.

Legend was made more than once that day, because it was said that Clara never screamed. Not once. But she did speak. She cursed her sister, her own lineage. She said since her sister let a man cause her to betray her blood, let her blood ever be without a man.

Everybody knew it would be so, because Clara died that night and a curse spoken before death always comes true.

As the years passed the story changed. For some reason a man often gets the credit for the glory—and the evil.

CHAPTER TWELVE

Evelyn and Deb dropped each other's hands as if they were hot coals. "You killed me," Deb whispered.

Evelyn felt drained and exhausted, but light in spirit. The circle had closed. The wrongs had finally been righted and the right choices made. She forgave and was forgiven.

"What the hell happened?" David sat heavily on the sofa, his eyes glazed. "Mass hallucination?"

"You know better, David." *Daniel, my Daniel,* her spirit sang. He was here with her finally, this time forever.

Deb sank to the floor, her shoulders heaving with silent sobs, and her face buried in her hands. Evelyn sat down beside her and stretched an arm across her shoulder.

"I never meant for…" Deb's voice trailed away. "I was mad and I just wasn't thinking. I was never thinking. That was my problem. I deserved to die. Forgive me, please forgive me."

"All is forgiven. Everything is all right now. Don't you understand? There's forgiveness instead of hate and vengeance, love instead of fear."

"Tell me what happened, Evelyn. I—I can't quite understand," David said, his face pained.

"The spirit never dies," she said. Evelyn stared at her hand. The skin, meat, sinew and bone. The beauty of it. "The body might be long crumbled into dust, but the spirit remains and in some sense the deeds of that person," she continued. "What Clara did resonated through time, trapping our spirits into an unfulfilling circle of dreams denied, jealousy, fear, and bitterness. This was the only time that the circle could be broken."

"Why now?"

"We've never been together before. This time and place brought our three spirits together. We had to touch. And to break the curse, Clara had to set things right. I had to set things right. I had to make the choices of love instead of fear, compassion instead of anger, and forgiveness instead of vengeance. Even if the situations were only a milder, shadowy sense of the tragedies that happened before, the ultimate choices are the same."

"Why did we remember?" Deb asked.

"The veil that separates us from the other side, and the memories of past lives that would overwhelm us, was ripped when we three connected at that particular time."

"I think that the memories were a gift also," David said.

"Why?" Evelyn asked.

"So we could remember the joy along with the pain." He gazed at Evelyn, his eyes full of love.

Then David looked at Deb. "So we could learn a lesson, change and grow."

Deb stood, and wiped the traces of tears from her cheeks. "Yes," she whispered, her voice husky with her own pain. "I'm sorry for coming over here and saying the things I did, David. It won't happen again. Evelyn—"

Evelyn met Deb's gaze. "It was jealousy. Not new jealousy over David, old jealousy. I've always envied your peace, your contentment, and how you always have people around who care about you. I'm sorry."

"I love you, Deb."

"I love you too, Evelyn." Then Deb turned and walked out the door, back into her new life.

Evelyn pulled a sweater over her shoulders before she walked out on their large deck overlooking the San Francisco Bay. The Golden Gate Bridge glittered in the background while glorious sunset colors played across the sky and burnished the mountaintops gold. This view from Mann County had to be one of the most breathtaking in the world, and it took her breath away every time she came out here.

She sat in the chair and took a sip of her lemonade. Now was the time to tell her husband. She scarcely finished her thought when he came out, carrying steaming brown paper bags that smelled heavenly.

"I made sure to order no MSG," David said, as he set the bags on the deck table and started to pull the cartons from the bags.

"Can we talk?" Evelyn asked.

David froze.

Evelyn chuckled. "I should have reworded the request. I remember how you once said those three words coming from a woman can strike terror within the breast of any man."

"And you said that you weren't just any woman. You were completely right."

She touched his hand and he sat down next to her. "What is it, Evelyn?"

"I'm going to have a baby."

Silence. Then David whooped so loud that Evelyn was sure that the folks in Oakland heard him.

"Sounds like you're happy about it," she said with a grin.

"Happy? I'm two powers squared past happy. Our child. Evelyn, we are finally going to have our child."

Evelyn nodded, happiness overflowing in her own heart. The circles of life turned and everything was as it should be. Such are the blessings that exist in the world.

☙❧

2009 Reprint Mass Market Titles

January

I'm Gonna Make You Love Me
Gwyneth Bolton
ISBN-13: 978-1-58571-291-5
ISBN-10: 1-58571-291-4
$6.99

Shades of Desire
Monica White
ISBN-13: 978-1-58571-292-2
ISBN-10: 1-58571-292-2
$6.99

February

A Love of Her Own
Cheris Hodges
ISBN-13: 978-1-58571-293-9
ISBN-10: 1-58571-293-0
$6.99

Color of Trouble
Dyanne Davis
ISBN-13: 978-1-58571-294-6
ISBN-10: 1-58571-096-6
$6.99

March

Twist of Fate
Beverly Clark
ISBN-13: 978-1-58571-295-3
ISBN-10: 1-58571-295-7
$6.99

Chances
Pamela Leigh Starr
ISBN-13: 978-1-58571-296-0
ISBN-10: 1-58571-296-5
$6.99

April

Sinful Intentions
Crystal Rhodes
ISBN-13: 978-1-585712-297-7
ISBN-10: 1-58571-297-3
$6.99

Rock Star
Roslyn Hardy Holcomb
ISBN-13: 978-1-58571-298-4
$6.99

May

Path of Fire
T.T. Henderson
ISBN-13: 978-1-58571-343-1
ISBN-10: 1-58571-343-0
$6.99

Caught Up in the Rapture
Lisa Riley
ISBN-13: 978-1-58571-344-8
ISBN-10: 1-58571-344-9
$6.99

June

Reckless Surrender
Rochelle Alers
ISBN-13: 978-1-58571-345-5
ISBN-10: 1-58571-345-7
$6.99

No Ordinary Love
Angela Weaver
ISBN-13: 978-1-58571-346-2
ISBN-10: 1-58571-346-5
$6.99

2009 Reprint Mass Market Titles (continued)

July

Intentional Mistakes
Michele Sudler
ISBN-13: 978-1-58571-347-9
ISBN-10: 1-58571-347-3
$6.99

It's in His Kiss
Reon Carter
ISBN-13: 978-1-58571-348-6
ISBN-10: 1-58571-348-1
$6.99

August

Unfinished Love Affair
Barbara Keaton
ISBN-13: 978-1-58571-349-3
ISBN-10: 1-58571-349-X
$6.99

A Perfect Place to Pray
I.L Goodwin
ISBN-13: 978-1-58571-299-1
ISBN-10: 1-58571-299-X
$6.99

September

Love in High Gear
Charlotte Roy
ISBN-13: 978-1-58571-355-4
ISBN-10: 1-58571-355-4
$6.99

Ebony Eyes
Kei Swanson
ISBN-13: 978-1-58571-356-1
ISBN-10: 1-58571-356-2
$6.99

October

Midnight Clear
Leslie Esdaile/Carmen Green
ISBN-13: 978-1-58571-357-8
ISBN-10: 1-58571-357-0
$6.99

Midnight Clear, Too
Gwynne Forster/Monica
  Jackson
ISBN-13: 978-1-58571-358-5
ISBN-10: 1-58571-358-9
$6.99

November

Midnight Peril
Vicki Andrews
ISBN-13: 978-1-58571-359-2
ISBN-10: 1-58571-359-7
$6.99

One Day at a Time
Bella McFarland
ISBN-13: 978-1-58571-360-8
ISBN-10: 1-58571-360-0
$6.99

December

Just an Affair
Eugenia O'Neal
ISBN-13: 978-1-58571-361-5
ISBN-10: 1-58571-361-9
$6.99

Shades of Brown
Denise Becker
ISBN-13: 978-1-58571-362-2
ISBN-10: 1-58571-362-7
$6.99

2009 New Mass Market Titles

January

Singing A Song…
Crystal Rhodes
ISBN-13: 978-1-58571-283-0
$6.99

Look Both Ways
Joan Early
ISBN-13: 978-1-58571-284-7
$6.99

February

Six O'Clock
Katrina Spencer
ISBN-13: 978-1-58571-285-4
$6.99

Red Sky
Renee Alexis
ISBN-13: 978-1-58571-286-1
$6.99

March

Anything But Love
Celya Bowers
ISBN-13: 978-1-58571-287-8
$6.99

Tempting Faith
Crystal Hubbard
ISBN-13: 978-1-58571-288-5
$6.99

April

If I Were Your Woman
LaConnie Taylor-Jones
ISBN-13: 978-1-58571-289-2
$6.99

Best of Luck Elsewhere
Trisha Haddad
ISBN-13: 978-1-58571-290-8
$6.99

May

All I'll Ever Need
Mildred Riley
ISBN-13: 978-1-58571-335-6
$6.99

A Place Like Home
Alicia Wiggins
ISBN-13: 978-1-58571-336-3
$6.99

June

Best Foot Forward
Michele Sudler
ISBN-13: 978-1-58571-337-0
$6.99

It's n the Rhythm
Sammie Ward
ISBN-13: 978-1-58571-338-7
$6.99

2009 New Mass Market Titles (continued)

July

Checks and Balances
Elaine Sims
ISBN-13: 978-1-58571-339-4
$6.99

Save Me
Africa Fine
ISBN-13: 978-1-58571-340-0
$6.99

August

When Lightening Strikes
Michele Cameron
ISBN-13: 978-1-58571-369-1
$6.99

Blindsided
Tammy Williams
ISBN-13: 978-1-58571-342-4
$6.99

September

2 Good
Celya Bowers
ISBN-13: 978-1-58571-350-9
$6.99

Waiting for Mr. Darcy
Chamein Canton
ISBN-13: 978-1-58571-351-6
$6.99

October

Fireflies
Joan Early
ISBN-13: 978-1-58571-352-3
$6.99

Frost On My Window
Angela Weaver
ISBN-13: 978-1-58571-353-0
$6.99

November

Waiting in the Shadows
Michele Sudler
ISBN-13: 978-1-58571-364-6
$6.99

Fixin' Tyrone
Keith Walker
ISBN-13: 978-1-58571-365-3
$6.99

December

Dream Keeper
Gail McFarland
ISBN-13: 978-1-58571-366-0
$6.99

Another Memory
Pamela Ridley
ISBN-13: 978-1-58571-367-7
$6.99

Other Genesis Press, Inc. Titles

Other Genesis Press, Inc. Titles (continued)

Other Genesis Press, Inc. Titles (continued)

Everything But Love	Natalie Dunbar	$8.95
Falling	Natalie Dunbar	$9.95
Fate	Pamela Leigh Starr	$8.95
Finding Isabella	A.J. Garrotto	$8.95
Forbidden Quest	Dar Tomlinson	$10.95
Forever Love	Wanda Y. Thomas	$8.95
From the Ashes	Kathleen Suzanne	$8.95
	Jeanne Sumerix	
Gentle Yearning	Rochelle Alers	$10.95
Glory of Love	Sinclair LeBeau	$10.95
Go Gentle Into That Good Night	Malcom Boyd	$12.95
Goldengroove	Mary Beth Craft	$16.95
Groove, Bang, and Jive	Steve Cannon	$8.99
Hand in Glove	Andrea Jackson	$9.95
Hard to Love	Kimberley White	$9.95
Hart & Soul	Angie Daniels	$8.95
Heart of the Phoenix	A.C. Arthur	$9.95
Heartbeat	Stephanie Bedwell-Grime	$8.95
Hearts Remember	M. Loui Quezada	$8.95
Hidden Memories	Robin Allen	$10.95
Higher Ground	Leah Latimer	$19.95
Hitler, the War, and the Pope	Ronald Rychiak	$26.95
How to Write a Romance	Kathryn Falk	$18.95
I Married a Reclining Chair	Lisa M. Fuhs	$8.95
I'll Be Your Shelter	Giselle Carmichael	$8.95
I'll Paint a Sun	A.J. Garrotto	$9.95
Icie	Pamela Leigh Starr	$8.95
Illusions	Pamela Leigh Starr	$8.95
Indigo After Dark Vol. I	Nia Dixon/Angelique	$10.95
Indigo After Dark Vol. II	Dolores Bundy/ Cole Riley	$10.95
Indigo After Dark Vol. III	Montana Blue/ Coco Morena	$10.95
Indigo After Dark Vol. IV	Cassandra Colt/	$14.95
Indigo After Dark Vol. V	Delilah Dawson	$14.95
Indiscretions	Donna Hill	$8.95
Intentional Mistakes	Michele Sudler	$9.95
Interlude	Donna Hill	$8.95

Other Genesis Press, Inc. Titles (continued)

Other Genesis Press, Inc. Titles (continued)

Other Genesis Press, Inc. Titles (continued)

Shades of Brown	Denise Becker	$8.95
Shades of Desire	Monica White	$8.95
Shadows in the Moonlight	Jeanne Sumerix	$8.95
Sin	Crystal Rhodes	$8.95
Small Whispers	Annetta P. Lee	$6.99
So Amazing	Sinclair LeBeau	$8.95
Somebody's Someone	Sinclair LeBeau	$8.95
Someone to Love	Alicia Wiggins	$8.95
Song in the Park	Martin Brant	$15.95
Soul Eyes	Wayne L. Wilson	$12.95
Soul to Soul	Donna Hill	$8.95
Southern Comfort	J.M. Jeffries	$8.95
Southern Fried Standards	S.R. Maddox	$6.99
Still the Storm	Sharon Robinson	$8.95
Still Waters Run Deep	Leslie Esdaile	$8.95
Stolen Memories	Michele Sudler	$6.99
Stories to Excite You	Anna Forrest/Divine	$14.95
Storm	Pamela Leigh Starr	$6.99
Subtle Secrets	Wanda Y. Thomas	$8.95
Suddenly You	Crystal Hubbard	$9.95
Sweet Repercussions	Kimberley White	$9.95
Sweet Sensations	Gwyneth Bolton	$9.95
Sweet Tomorrows	Kimberly White	$8.95
Taken by You	Dorothy Elizabeth Love	$9.95
Tattooed Tears	T. T. Henderson	$8.95
The Color Line	Lizzette Grayson Carter	$9.95
The Color of Trouble	Dyanne Davis	$8.95
The Disappearance of Allison Jones	Kayla Perrin	$5.95
The Fires Within	Beverly Clark	$9.95
The Foursome	Celya Bowers	$6.99
The Honey Dipper's Legacy	Myra Pannell-Allen	$14.95
The Joker's Love Tune	Sidney Rickman	$15.95
The Little Pretender	Barbara Cartland	$10.95
The Love We Had	Natalie Dunbar	$8.95
The Man Who Could Fly	Bob & Milana Beamon	$18.95
The Missing Link	Charlyne Dickerson	$8.95
The Mission	Pamela Leigh Starr	$6.99
The More Things Change	Chamein Canton	$6.99

Other Genesis Press, Inc. Titles (continued)

Order Form

Mail to: Genesis Press, Inc.
P.O. Box 101
Columbus, MS 39703

Name _____
Address _____
City/State _____ Zip _____
Telephone _____

Ship to (if different from above)
Name _____
Address _____
City/State _____ Zip _____
Telephone _____

Credit Card Information
Credit Card # _____ ☐ Visa ☐ Mastercard
Expiration Date (mm/yy) _____ ☐ AmEx ☐ Discover

Qty.	Author	Title	Price	Total

Use this order form, or call
1-888-INDIGO-1

Total for books _____
Shipping and handling:
  $5 first two books,
  $1 each additional book _____
Total S & H _____
Total amount enclosed _____
Mississippi residents add 7% sales tax